'It's terrific stuff . . . classily put together and lip-smackingly gory.' *Financial Times*

'Bound to be popular with boys . . . this is a skilful, intelligent thriller.' *The Times*

Praise for *The Dreamwalker's Child*:

Steve Voake's debut, *The Dreamwalker's Child*, is an ingenious and fast-paced thriller . . . his book buzzes and hums with ideas.' *The Times*

Praise for *The Web of Fire*:

A compelling sequel.' *The Times*

Praise for *The Starlight Conspiracy*:

It's been a while since anything as much fun as Steve Voake's *The Starlight Conspiracy* came along . . . The quality of the writing, and the heart-warming sympathy it evokes makes this a really good, thought-provoking and exciting choice.' *The Times*

FIGHTBACK

Steve Voake grew up in Midsomer Norton, near Bath. Before becoming a full-time writer, Steve was headteacher of a village school in Somerset. He is the critically acclaimed author of *The Dreamwalker's Child*, *The Web of Fire*, *The Starlight Conspiracy* and *Blood Hunters*. He lives with his family in Somerset.

by the same author:

The Dreamwalker's Child
The Web of Fire
The Starlight Conspiracy
Blood Hunters

STEVE VOAKE

FIGHTBACK

ff

faber and faber

First published in 2010
by Faber and Faber Limited
Bloomsbury House,
74–77 Great Russell Street,
London WC1B 3DA

Typeset by RefineCatch Limited, Bungay, Suffolk
Printed in England by CPI Bookmarque, Croydon

A CIP record for this book
is available from the British Library

ISBN 978–0–571–23003–7

2 4 6 8 10 9 7 5 3 1

ONE

'I'm sorry I missed it,' said his father as they made their way out of the brightly lit hall. 'Something came up.'

Kier stuffed the trophy into his bag, along with his gumshield and karate suit.

'It doesn't matter,' he said.

When they got into the car, his father was the first to break the silence.

'I hear he was a tough opponent.'

'Yeah.'

'But you were tougher?'

Kier shrugged. The final jump-kick had been a risk which nearly disqualified him. But, after some discussion, the judges had ruled that it was controlled enough to win him three points and the tournament. His father had missed it of course, same as he missed everything else.

'I guess I just hated him more than he hated me.'

His father turned in his seat, studying him in the half-light.

'What do you mean?'

'My instructor told me the secret of winning is to hate your opponent. He said it was the only way to be the best.'

'Well, he's wrong about that.'

It was raining now; people were running across the car park, silhouetted against the sky.

'Love is stronger than hate, Kier. Find out what matters, that's the real secret. Find out and go after it the best way you can.'

Yeah, right, thought Kier. *Maybe you could have come after me once in a while.*

As they listened to the rain drumming on the roof, his father wiped a patch of steam from the windscreen with his sleeve.

'Listen, Kier, I'm sorry I've not been around much these past few years. But you know, when your mum died, with my job and everything, I didn't really have a choice.'

For a moment, Kier allowed himself to think about how the man sitting next to him could have been someone he knew. But when the other kids had gone home from boarding school for the holidays he had been left watching dust dance in the sunlit hall, waiting for the taxis and planes that would take him away; off to the summer camps and ski camps where he would swim and trek over mountains with strangers, trying not to think about what might have been.

Kier shrugged.

'Lots of parents send their kids away to school,' he said. 'It's no big deal.'

For a moment it seemed as if his father was about to say more. But then he just rubbed his eyes, turned the key in the ignition and drove in silence towards the exit.

Kier checked the passport in his pocket, knowing that tomorrow the awkwardness would be over and they would be miles apart once more. Closing his eyes, he listened to the clunk of the wipers and the hiss of tyres in the rain.

He awoke to the roar of engines as the car swerved violently to the left, making him bang his head against the side window. A car horn blared and wet tarmac glistened in the glare of headlights.

'Stupid idiot,' said his father, hands gripping the wheel. 'What the hell does he think he's doing?'

Kier turned to see a white van drawing alongside them. The passenger pointed through the window and then the van veered sharply to the left, smashing into the side of their car. They slid across two lanes of motorway, Kier watching his father wrestle with the wheel as they skidded along the hard shoulder in a squeal of smoking rubber. They finally came to rest with a loud thump against the side of the embankment and the white van pulled over, parking at an angle in front of them.

'Bloody maniac,' said his father angrily, releasing his seat belt. He turned off the engine and wrenched the car door open. As he walked along the hard shoulder towards the van, Kier watched in a daze as the van door slowly opened. Suddenly his father was running back towards the car again, his face white as he threw himself into the driver's seat.

'What's the matter?' Kier asked, watching him fumble with the keys.

'We have to go,' replied his father.

Then the windscreen dissolved in a hot, blinding roar and Kier felt a rush of air as the back window blew out. Suddenly he was staring through a glitter of broken glass at a hooded man with a pump-action shotgun. As the man took aim again, Kier's father floored the accelerator and the back seat exploded, fragments of foam and leather spinning off into the night.

As they accelerated away, Kier turned to look through the shattered window and saw the two men running back towards the van.

'Who were they?' he asked, unable to believe what had just happened.

But his father didn't seem to hear.

'I think I need a hospital,' he said, and when Kier glanced over he saw that his father's shirt was soaked in blood.

'What can I do?' Kier asked.

His father shook his head.

'You have to run,' he said. 'When we get to the hospital, you have to run and not look back.'

TWO

'It's going to be all right,' Kier reassured him as they drove through the hospital entrance, 'everything's going to be all right.'

But as the car mounted the central roundabout and came to rest in the middle of some flowerbeds, Kier's father slumped over the wheel and closed his eyes as if, having done enough to get him there, his body was incapable of anything more.

Kier kicked the door open and tumbled out on to the sloping earth, running as fast as he could towards the entrance. Two paramedics emerged, off-duty and smiling at the thought of the evening ahead.

'Help me,' said Kier, grabbing one of them by the sleeve. 'Please. You have to help me.'

They were quick, efficient and professional. Kier walked with the trolley as they pushed his father along the corridor, holding his hand as he slipped in and out of consciousness.

'Kier,' said his father weakly, trying to raise his head from the pillow.

'Shh,' said Kier. 'Don't try to talk.'

'No police,' whispered his father. 'Spike Russell. Fern behind a fox . . . it's great . . . Russell's treat . . . dead . . .'

'Dead?'

'Dead . . . drop . . . dead . . .'

As his father closed his eyes, one of the medics shook his head and gave Kier a sympathetic glance. 'It's OK. He's delirious. He doesn't know what he's saying.'

They took him to an emergency room full of machines and surgical instruments. Kier could hear how quickly and urgently the doctors spoke, giving one another careful instructions.

Then the door closed and Kier was left to watch porters push clanking trolleys along the brightly lit corridor. After ten minutes the door opened and a young nurse emerged, wiping her hands on the front of her apron.

'I'm sorry,' she said, as if it was her fault, crouching in front of him and taking both his hands in hers. 'There was nothing more we could do.'

Kier nodded, numb with shock as he realised that the father he hardly knew was dead. His world was crumbling, dissolving before his eyes.

'Is there anyone we can contact? Someone who can take you home?'

'No.' Kier shook his head. 'There's no one.'

He stared past the nurse's shoulder and saw two men at the far end of the corridor, their faces concealed beneath the dark hoods of their jackets. They were stopping at each of the wards, looking in and checking the beds. As Kier watched, one of them turned to stare at him. He nudged the other man, who looked up and nodded. Then Kier was on his feet and running, the sound of clattering footsteps echoing down the corridor behind him.

He cannoned through some double doors and sent a startled nurse stumbling against the wall. Dodging a porter with a trolley, he thumped through a second set of doors and skidded round the corner, bouncing off the wall and jumping down a flight of stairs. Momentarily winded, he bent to get his breath and heard voices approaching. As he grasped the banister and swung himself round on to the next stairway, there was a muffled crack and a bullet ricocheted off the handrail, whining past his ear like a hungry mosquito.

It was a bad dream, a nightmare, except that he was wide awake in the middle of an ordinary hospital and someone was trying to kill him.

Kier's heart raced and his muscles cried out for

oxygen. But adrenalin kept him moving, sharpening his senses and helping him make the decisions that could save his life.

Swinging around on to the final set of steps, he heard the deep thump of a shotgun blast and then the huge picture window in front of him disintegrated, sending shards of glass spinning down into the car park below. Clearing the last four steps in a single jump, he hit the floor and crashed through the doors in front of him. To his left was a small cafe with a handful of late-night visitors sipping their lattes and flicking through the day's news. To the right was a long empty corridor leading to the main entrance.

Logic told him he would never make it.

Fear screamed at him to go.

As the entrance doors slid open, he stumbled out into fresh air just as the first bullet struck the edge of the frame with a noise like a hammer on steel. The second missed his ankle by a millimetre, burying itself deep in the tarmac. As Kier ran across the access road a taxi screeched to a halt and the driver leaned on his horn, swearing at him through the open window. But Kier wasn't stopping for anyone; as another bullet punched through the *Give Way* sign, he leapt over a low picket fence and into a small patch of woodland.

'There he is!' shouted a voice. 'Over there!'

With a *prrrrrp* like sackcloth being torn in half, a hail of bullets ripped through the leaves and branches, exploding bark from tree trunks and kicking up the earth around his feet.

A machine gun?

This was in*sane*.

Ahead, through the trees, Kier could see the main road. Reaching the edge of the woodland, he vaulted the fence, almost colliding with an old woman waiting to cross at the lights. As the lights turned green, a white pick-up truck began to pull away and Kier leapt into the back, throwing himself headlong on to a pile of bricks and plasterboard. He lay there for several minutes, breathing in dust as the truck rumbled on. At the third set of lights he jumped down and sat by the side of the road, staring at a patch of oil and wondering if he would live to see another morning.

THREE

He caught the last tube home and watched neon-lit stations slip past as if in a dream. The world seemed unreal, as if he were merely playing a part in a film. But Kier knew that this was just the body's way of dealing with shock. The world was real and dangerous. And whoever had killed his father wanted to kill him too.

He took the precaution of leaving the train one stop early, walking the rest of the way. When he reached his father's road he stayed in the shadows, looking for signs that someone might be waiting for him. But the street was quiet and deserted.

For now at least, it seemed that he was safe.

No police, his father had said. *Spike Russell, fern behind a fox . . . it's great . . .* Were his father's last words really the ramblings of a delirious mind, as the medic had said? Or had he been trying to tell him something important?

Kier slotted the key into the lock and stood

motionless in the hallway, listening for the slightest whisper or creak of the floorboards. But all he could hear was the ticking of the grandfather clock and the beating of his heart. He was about to switch the hall light on when it occurred to him that this might not be such a good idea. Instead he shut the door and moved upstairs to his father's study, opening the blinds enough to let the moonlight filter through into the room.

His father's Filofax lay open on the desk next to the laptop. He flicked through the addresses but there was no sign of anyone called Spike Russell. Opening the laptop, Kier signed into the guest account and entered *Spike Russell* into the search engine. There were a few links to Facebook sites and an entry about a character in a film, but nothing gave any useful clues. He wasn't even sure what he hoped to find. He tried *fern behind a fox*, but that just came up with a list of garden centres. And hadn't his father said something about a treat? It didn't make any sense.

Dead . . . drop dead . . .

That was the other thing he'd said.

Maybe the medic was right after all. Maybe his dad was just delirious.

Maybe he would just type it in anyway.

As he expected, a whole list of results came up. A couple of recent movies, a line of clothing called 'Drop Dead Gorgeous', an explanation of the phrase in some online free dictionary. There was even an entry for a Christian Death Metal Band. But nothing of any use to him. Without much hope, Kier clicked on the next page.

Still nothing.

He clicked again.

And suddenly, there it was:

```
Dead Drop: Information from
Answers.com
A prearranged spot at which one
party passes information to
another without actually meeting;
or, the act of making such a
transfer, as in 'making a dead
drop'.
```

Kier stared at the screen. Could this be what his father had meant?

He cleared the search engine and typed 'dead drop'.

This time it was right there in the very first entry:

A dead drop or dead letter box is
a location used to secretly pass
items between two people, without
requiring them to meet.

At the bottom of the page was a picture of a
long, sharp object. Underneath it said:

Dead drop spike. A dead drop spike
is a concealment device used to
hide money, maps, documents,
microfilms and other items. The
spike is waterproof and can be
pushed into the ground or placed
in a shallow stream to be
retrieved at a later time.

Kier sat back in the chair and looked at the moonlight filtering through the blinds.

So that was what his father had been trying to tell
him. *It's great . . . Russell's treat.* Suddenly it was
blindingly obvious. There was no one called Spike
Russell waiting around with a treat. But maybe
there was a dead drop spike. And maybe, just
maybe, it was hidden somewhere in Great Russell
Street . . .

He was about to search for a map of the area

when his fingers froze above the keyboard.

The sound from downstairs was faint but un-mistakable.

It was the sound of breaking glass.

In his panic, potential hiding places flashed through his mind – under the bed perhaps, in the attic. But he knew these people didn't mess around. If he hid anywhere in the house, they would find him.

And if they found him, they would kill him.

Moving silently on the balls of his feet, Kier picked up his father's high-backed chair and wedged it beneath the door handle before opening the window and peering down into the back garden. There was a thin strip of lawn and a few flowerbeds, but he was two floors up and a straight jump would almost certainly earn him a broken ankle.

He turned to see the door handle moving.

There was a creak from the floorboards and a voice whispered, 'He's here.'

Then, as the frame splintered around the hinges, Kier clambered out through the window and leapt sideways on to a honeysuckle-covered trellis.

Perhaps if he had been lighter, the trellis might have held. But muscle weighs more than fat, and the twice-weekly karate training sessions meant muscles formed a major part of Kier's body. Good news if you were entering a karate tournament; not so good if you were hanging by your fingers from a piece of wood.

Kier heard the timber crack and saw the screws pop out of the brickwork before the trellis peeled away from the wall and he landed heavily in the flowerbeds, still clutching fragments of wood and honeysuckle in his fists. Scrambling to his feet, he brushed earth from his jeans and ran to the gate at the end of the garden. Beyond the gate was an alleyway which he knew would take him past the back gardens and into the road again. Glancing around, he saw two figures silhouetted against the window and decided there was no time to waste. Sliding the bolt back, he pulled the gate open and ran out into the alley.

He should have known, of course.

Should have realised that he was dealing with professionals who wouldn't make the basic mistake of leaving an obvious escape route open. With an almost imperceptible movement of his wrist, the man in the black tracksuit palmed the handle of the six-inch knife and smiled.

'Going somewhere?' he said.

In the movies, the bad guy usually raises his knife above his head so that the hero can step in and do some fancy kung-fu work. Luckily for Kier, his karate instructor had known that real life isn't like the movies.

'He won't advertise,' he had told him. 'If he's got a knife, he'll come at you fast and hard and the first you'll know about it is when he buries it in your guts. So watch and learn.'

Kier had watched and learned, and this gave him two distinct advantages. One: he was expecting the attack. Two: his attacker thought that killing him was going to be easy.

As the man lunged forward, Kier turned and thrust his left arm up beneath the man's out-stretched right arm. Clamping his free hand down on the man's wrist, he twisted hard, swept his foot beneath the man's legs and slammed him down on to the concrete path. Although it was a move he had practised many times, Kier was still relieved to see how easily the man went down. But he wasn't taking any chances. As the man struggled to his feet, Kier jumped up and scissor-kicked him back into some dustbins.

'And *stay* down,' he said.

Then, as the neighbourhood dogs began to howl, he turned and ran for his life.

FOUR

By the time he got off the tube at Russell Square it was past midnight and Kier was exhausted. As he took the lift and walked out into the empty street, the reality of what had happened began to sink in. The father he barely knew had been murdered in front of him. For some reason, his father hadn't wanted him to go to the police. And now the men who had killed him obviously wanted Kier dead too.

He was hungry and thirsty, with no money and no idea what to do. All he had was a vague idea that there was some kind of spike buried somewhere in Great Russell Street. It was crazy. But then, watching your father get killed and having to run for your life was pretty crazy too.

Fern behind a fox . . .

Kier sat on the wall outside the British Museum and looked up and down the road. Opposite him was a row of shops, all closed of course – a bookshop, a shop selling souvenirs of London, but no sign of any foxes or ferns.

He turned and peered through the railings that surrounded the museum, but everywhere was stone and concrete except for a large rectangle of grass in the centre. Hardly the kind of place someone would choose to bury a secret spike. Turning his attention back to the street, Kier decided his best hope was to check around the base of the trees which grew along the pavement. Although the earth around them was covered in gravel and pale dust, there was at least a possibility that something could be buried there. No sign of any ferns of course, but Kier guessed he'd have to work with what he had.

It was only after scuffing his foot unsuccessfully around the base of the seventh tree that he saw it.

A hundred metres or so down on the other side of the road.

Trees.

Lots of them.

Trees, bushes and grass.

A park.

Standing outside the railings, Kier saw that, apart from an old man sleeping on a bench, the park was deserted. To his right was a small children's playground with a plastic slide and some painted animals on springs. There was a black and white cow, a duck and a sheep. But no fox. At the front of the park was a statue of some old guy in a toga and sandals. Behind him, to the left of the path, was a circular patch of ground surrounded by a waist-high beech hedge. Kier could see that there were several flowerbeds surrounding a paved area in the middle of the park. He guessed if there was a spike, it could be in any one of them. If it was there at all. He stood for a moment, watching the red tail lights of late-night taxis and wondering if he was wasting his time. Then he looked at the statue again and saw that there were three words written in the middle of the plinth. The words said: CHARLES JAMES FOX.

Thirty seconds later, Kier was climbing through the beech hedge and staring at the shade-loving plants that grew beneath the tree in the centre. Pushing their way up through the groundcover of geraniums and ivy and foxgloves were three large ferns, shaped like green shuttlecocks.

Kier felt the tips of his fingers tingle.

Fern behind a fox . . .

This was it. This was the place.

Getting down on his hands and knees, he began to crawl around, searching for any signs that the ground might have been disturbed. But the soil was soft and deep, layers of rich, dark earth spread out beneath the plants. As he raked methodically through it with his fingers, Kier remembered how he used to plunge his hands into the lucky dip at school fairs, trembling with excitement at the thought of what he might find.

He was trembling now, but for very different reasons.

Moving to the last of the ferns, Kier dragged his fingers through the soil once more and almost immediately felt his middle finger snag on something. Brushing away the earth, he saw a loop of plastic protruding from the earth. It came out easily, bringing with it a black plastic tube the size of a toilet roll.

On the end of the tube was a spike.

Kier whistled softly.

'Jackpot,' he said.

Unscrewing the cap, he pulled out a thick roll of fifty-pound notes. He guessed there had to be several thousand pounds' worth. Stuffing the money into his pocket, he held up the tube and peered inside, but there was nothing else.

No note, no clue.

No nothing.

'Damn it.' Kier threw the empty tube into the bushes, sat back and wiped his hands on his jeans.

Although he was a good deal richer than he had been thirty seconds ago, he was no closer to finding an answer. But at least now he could check himself into a hotel, take a hot shower and get a good night's sleep without some nutcase trying to blow his head off.

He stood up, stretched, then suddenly his legs buckled and he was face down staring at the dirt.

'Don't move,' hissed a voice, 'or I'll tear your throat out.'

As if being thrown to the ground wasn't enough of a surprise, Kier now had to take in the fact that the person kneeling on his back sounded very much like a girl.

'Get off me,' he said, twisting his head around.

For the second time that night, he found himself staring at the point of a knife.

'Do that again and you'll regret it.'

Kier turned his head back until he was looking at the trunk of the tree.

'OK,' he said wearily. 'I won't do that again.'

'Why are you here?'

The voice definitely belonged to a girl. A strong one, too. Probably one of those bodybuilder types.

'I dropped some money.'

'Liar.'

As the grip tightened around his neck, Kier

stared at the earth and tried not to think about the knife.

'It's true, I swear.'

Well, it *was* true, in a way. He had dropped some money once. A couple of years ago.

'How much?'

'Oh, I dunno. Couple of quid.'

'You expect me to believe you were grubbing around in a park at two in the morning for the sake of a couple of quid?'

She obviously wasn't convinced.

'Look, I'm short of money, OK? I can't afford to lose two quid.'

'Is that so?'

The girl thrust her hand in his pocket and dropped the bundle of notes in front of his face.

'So you're short of money, eh?'

Kier suddenly felt very tired.

'Look, just take it, OK? I don't want it. It's yours.'

'I know it's mine. But what I want to know is, how did you know it was there?'

Kier closed his eyes and decided he couldn't keep this up any more. And he really, really didn't want to get killed.

'My dad told me,' he said.

'Your *dad*?' The girl sounded genuinely surprised.

'Yes, my dad. Something bad happened to him,

OK? I guess he must have wanted me to have it or something.'

'What's your dad's name?'

'David. His name was David West.'

Kier felt the pressure release on his neck. When he turned around, he was surprised to see a petite girl of about sixteen kneeling in the earth beside him. Beneath the curtain of dark, glossy hair, a pair of emerald-green eyes widened in the half-light.

'My God,' she said. 'You must be Kier.'

FIVE

'How do you know my name?' asked Kier.

The girl shrugged. 'Your dad spoke about you sometimes,' she said. 'I think he wished he could see you more often.'

Kier stared at her, this stranger who seemed to know more about his father than he did. She stared right back at him and Kier could see a fierceness there, a steel in her eyes that helped him understand how she had floored him so easily.

'He told you that?'

'He didn't have to.' She folded the knife and slipped it back into the pocket of her blue corduroy jacket. 'You said something bad happened to him.'

'Yeah. He kind of . . . died.'

The girl took a sharp intake of breath and, as she ran her fingers through her hair, Kier saw that she was genuinely upset.

'What happened?'

Kier thought about the bizarre direction his life was taking. Sitting in a park in the middle of the night, talking to a strange girl who not five minutes ago had knocked him down and threatened to kill him.

'Why don't you tell me? I mean, since you seem to know so much about him.'

The girl nodded.

'Maybe later. But from what you say, I think we should probably get moving.'

Kier frowned.

'Who *are* you?'

For the first time since they met, the girl almost smiled.

'I'm Saskia,' she said, sticking out her hand. 'Pleased to meet you, Kier.'

This was certainly an interesting way of doing things, thought Kier. Attack someone and then introduce yourself as if you're at a dinner party. But he took her hand and shook it anyway.

'Likewise, I guess.'

He let go of her hand and wiped dirt from his forehead.

'So, Saskia. Are you going to tell me what's going on?'

Saskia nodded.

'Yes. But not here.'

She picked up the bundle of notes and put them in her pocket.

'You look as though you could do with getting cleaned up. Maybe we should get a hotel for the night.'

Kier raised an eyebrow. 'I hardly know you.'

'I meant *separate* rooms,' said Saskia.

But when Kier looked at her, he saw that she was smiling.

He was woken the next morning by a knock on the door.

'It's me, Saskia. Meet you for breakfast in fifteen minutes.'

Kier was relieved and somewhat surprised. She had refused to talk to him last night, telling him he needed to get some rest. He had half-expected to find her gone this morning. But, well, here she was.

'OK,' he said to the door. 'See you there.'

Stumbling across to the window, he pulled back the curtains to reveal a beautiful blue sky. Looking out at the streets bathed in sunshine, it was hard to believe that the events of yesterday could have happened. It felt like a horrible dream. But as he looked at the bruises on his legs, he knew it was true. His father *had* been murdered and he *had* jumped from a second-floor window to escape from his killers. And now he was about to have breakfast with a girl whose idea of a polite introduction was to shove your face in the dirt.

In the shower he allowed himself to cry for the first time, tipping his head back and letting the water wash away his tears. But the years away from home had taught him to stay strong. After five minutes, he climbed out and splashed his face with cold water until the redness around his eyes disappeared.

'OK,' he said. 'That's it. No more.'

Saskia was sitting at a table by the window, coolly sipping her orange juice as if staying in fancy hotels and fighting with strangers was part of her everyday routine.

'Morning,' she said as Kier sat opposite her. 'Hungry?'

'Starving.'

She nodded towards the self-service buffet.

'Then eat.'

Kier returned with bacon and eggs and looked at the people out on the terrace. They were all smiling and enjoying the sunshine, believing that the world was a safe and wonderful place.

'So,' said Kier. 'Are you going to tell me?'

'I think,' said Saskia, carefully spreading honey

on her toast, 'I'd better leave that to someone else.'

'Someone else? What do you mean?'

Saskia looked around to make sure no waiters were hovering within earshot.

'I had to make a phone call last night. Just to check you're who you say you are. And to find out what they want me to do.'

'They?' Kier was getting frustrated now. 'Who are they?'

'Shhh,' said Saskia. 'Keep your voice down.'

Kier leaned across the table and lowered his voice.

'Who are they?'

'The people your dad worked for. The people I work for.' Saskia finished her orange juice and placed the empty glass on her plate. 'And the people you're going to work for too.'

'Me?'

'Uh-huh.'

'Oh no. No way.' Kier balled up his paper napkin and pushed his chair back. 'You know what? Forget it. I'm going.'

'Going?' Saskia raised her eyebrows and regarded him dispassionately across the table. 'Going where exactly?'

She was right, of course. He had nowhere to go.

'I don't know. Back to school.'

'You're on holiday, remember? And anyway, who do you think pays your fees?'

Kier stared at her, unable to believe what he was hearing.

'Please, Kier, sit down.' She nodded towards the waiter. 'Just relax. Here comes your coffee.'

Kier sat down and took a sip of espresso.

'I don't understand any of this,' he said.

'Of course you don't,' said Saskia, pushing the remains of her toast to one side. 'But you should know that these men, the ones who came after your dad – they're bad people. Very bad.'

'You don't say.' Kier took another sip of his coffee. 'I kind of figured that one out for myself.'

'Yeah, but the thing is, Kier, there are lots of them, all working together. And they'll get rid of anyone who stands in their way.'

'But I'm not standing in their way. I'm running as fast as I can in the opposite direction.'

'Ah, but you've seen them, haven't you? They're not going to risk the fact you might be able to identify them. It's easier for them just to kill you too.'

'But it was dark and they had their hoods up. I'd never be able to identify them.'

Saskia shrugged.

'You mean they'd kill me anyway? That's crazy.'

'I know.' Saskia licked honey from her fingers and wiped them on a napkin. 'Welcome to my world, Kier.'

Kier stared at her, this small, neatly dressed girl sitting opposite him with her blue corduroy jacket and expensive haircut, and for a moment he wondered if she was some kind of nut-job. But she'd known about his dad, hadn't she? And despite her innocent appearance, she could fight like a tiger. He watched her fold up her napkin and lay her cutlery neatly on top of it.

'So what is your world, Saskia? And where exactly do you fit into all this?'

'Let's just say I work for one of the good guys.'

'Oh yeah, and who's that? Batman?'

'No, just someone who doesn't like the way the world's turning out. Someone with enough time and money to do something about it.'

'Which is how my father got killed?'

'Standing up for what you believe in is a high-risk business, Kier.'

'Is that why you do it? Risk your life because you believe it's right?'

'Partly.' Saskia smiled and patted her pocket. 'And partly because the pay's pretty good.'

'I don't get it. What are you saying, exactly?'

'I'm saying that you need to have all this properly explained. And here is not the place to talk about it. Besides, we really need to get your passport.'

Kier frowned.

'My passport? Why?'

'Because we're going on a trip. You do *have* a passport, right?'

'You mean like this?' As they walked out of the dining room, Kier reached into his pocket and pulled out a little red booklet. Noticing Saskia's puzzled look he added, 'I needed it to prove my identity for the British Karate Tournament.'

Saskia smiled and pressed the button for the lift.

'I think you're going to like your new job,' she said. 'It's got your name written all over it.'

SIX

It was nine-thirty by the time they took the Piccadilly Line westbound from Russell Square, heading for Victoria. Their carriage was unusually empty: Kier assumed the rush hour must be over, while tourists were still eating their breakfast.

'Is it far?' he asked. 'I haven't even got a tooth-brush.'

'Relax,' said Saskia. 'We'll sort everything out once we get there.'

'Get where?'

'Crete.'

'*Crete?* What are we going to Crete for?'

'You'll like it. It's sunny.'

'It's sunny here.'

'Not as sunny as Crete. Besides, there's no one there who wants to kill you. At least, not as far as I know.'

'Thanks. That makes me feel a lot better.'

The train stopped at Holborn and three men

got on. They were all in their late teens or early twenties, all wearing red football shirts, tracksuit bottoms and trainers. Although the carriage was empty, the largest of the three came and sat directly opposite Saskia. Kier noticed he had the flattened nose of a boxer and Union Jack flags tattooed on both fists. The other two sat next to him, staring at Kier without a word. As the train pulled out of the station, Tattoo Man folded his arms, grinned and winked at Saskia.

'Hello, darling,' he said. 'You all right?'

'I'm fine, thank you,' said Saskia. 'And just so as you know – I'm not your darling.'

'Aww,' said Tattoo Man, still smiling. 'And there was me gonna ask you out on a date.'

'No offence,' replied Saskia coolly, 'but I think I'd rather chew my arm off.'

The man's smile vanished and the other two guys stared at him, waiting to see what he would do next.

'You think you're pretty smart, don't you?'

Saskia didn't say anything.

Good, thought Kier. *Maybe if she shuts up we'll get out of here in one piece.*

The man leaned forward and put his hand on Saskia's leg.

'This is nice,' he said, stroking the material. 'Did your daddy buy it for you?'

34

'Look,' said Kier, 'why don't you just leave her alone?'

Without warning, the man leapt from his seat and grabbed Kier by the throat.

'You shut your mouth,' he hissed, squeezing until Kier began to choke. 'Shut your mouth while I talk to my friend here, or I'm going to spread you all over this carriage. Understand?'

Kïer nodded, gasping for breath.

'Yeah, I understand.'

As the man shoved him roughly back in his seat, Kier knew they were in serious trouble. The guy was a hundred and sixty pounds of solid muscle and Saskia had made him look stupid in front of his mates. Now, by the look in his eyes, someone was definitely going to pay for it.

'Stay calm, OK?' Saskia whispered. 'Don't do anything.'

'What did you say?' asked the man.

'I told him not to worry,' said Saskia. 'I told him everything was going to be all right.'

The man smiled nastily.

'Is that what you think? You think everything's going to be all right?'

Saskia shrugged.

'Usually works for me.'

'Well, not this time, darling. This time, I'm

gonna teach you and your friend some manners.'

They sat in silence until the next stop, which was Covent Garden. Saskia tapped Kier on the shoulder and they made their way out on to the platform, but Kier felt his stomach lurch as the three men followed them. There were four lifts, and as they got into the first one, a woman began shepherding her two children in.

'Sorry,' said Tattoo Man, stepping forward and standing in the doorway. 'This one's full.'

As the door slid shut, he looked at Kier and squeezed his knuckles until they cracked.

'Are you scared?' he asked.

'After the day I had yesterday,' said Kier, 'not really, no.'

He was lying, of course. Inside, his stomach was turning to mush. But he wasn't going to let them see it.

Saskia winked at him and he guessed she didn't realise he was about to get the beating of his life. But he wasn't going down without a fight. If he could just keep Tattoo Man and his friends occupied for a couple of minutes, then at least Saskia might have the chance to run away. But as the man stepped forward and raised his fists, Kier knew it was going to hurt.

A lot.

'Wait,' said Saskia, tapping Tattoo Man on the shoulder and stopping him in his tracks. 'Can you teach me first?'

The man scowled and turned around.

'What?'

'You were going to teach us some manners,' Saskia explained, 'and I want you to teach me first.'

Before he had time to react, Saskia went into a crouch and then there was a blur of movement, so fast and smooth it was almost impossible to tell what was happening. One moment she was leaning against the lift wall, the next she was bouncing between the three men as if they were posts in a pinball machine. Kier stood back and watched in amazement as she jumped and twirled, legs flailing and arms pumping like small jackhammers. Then, as quickly as it had begun, it was over and Saskia stood in the middle of the lift with her arms by her sides, the three men groaning on the floor around her. Kier noticed that her breathing was calm and relaxed, as if she had just popped out for a carton of milk.

'That's better,' she said as the doors opened. 'Now I feel much more polite.'

Kier stared in disbelief, first at her and then at the semi-conscious men on the floor behind them.

'I don't understand,' he said as they hurried back down the stairs towards the platform. 'What just happened?'

'Well, I could hardly do it on the train,' said Saskia. 'They've got CCTV cameras everywhere. I had to make sure we went somewhere a bit more . . . private.'

'No, I mean what *happened*? How did you do that?'

'Do what?' Saskia seemed genuinely puzzled.

'You know. In the lift. Knocking them all out.'

'Oh, *that*,' she said dismissively, as if merely discussing the best way to swat a fly. 'People like that are always easy. They don't have any idea what they're dealing with.'

As they waited on the platform for the next train to arrive, Kier looked at the small, dark-haired girl standing next to him and shook his head.

'What exactly *are* they dealing with?' he asked.

Saskia turned to him and smiled.

'That's what you're about to find out,' she said.

SEVEN

They took the Gatwick Express from Victoria station and once they arrived at the airport Saskia bought their plane tickets over the counter.

'I didn't know they let you pay in cash,' said Kier.

Saskia shrugged.

'Usually means you attract a bit more attention, but if anyone asks, just say you're staying with me.' She smiled. 'I always check out beautifully on their computer.'

The departure hall was full of bright lights and shops selling duty-free goods. It felt like no man's land, a place where people's lives were put on hold while the rest of the world just kept on spinning

'I think I need a coffee,' said Kier.

'Coffee's bad for you,' said Saskia. 'Didn't you know that?'

'So is getting your head blown off,' replied Kier. 'But I know which I prefer.'

★ ★ ★

Later, as the plane accelerated down the runway, Kier thought how strange it was the way life changed direction when you least expected it. He had taken it for granted that the next few years were pretty much mapped out for him: studying for exams, practising his karate, playing football beneath grey winter skies and trying to work out what he would one day become. But now everything had changed and his old life was falling away, leaving only a strange, bright emptiness inside.

As he stared out of the window at the clouds piled up like fields of freshly fallen snow, he imagined himself walking across them, never looking back, making footprints in places he had never been before.

He thanked the air stewardess and followed Saskia out on to the aircraft steps. After the cool, air-conditioned interior of the plane, the heat hit him like a blast furnace, bringing with it a strange cocktail of scents: sweat, dust, oil and the sweet aromatic fragrance of thyme, carried across parched fields on a warm summer wind.

'Welcome to Crete,' said Saskia as they walked through passport control.

Through the huge picture windows of the arrivals hall, Kier saw the heat haze shimmering on the tarmac and the dry, brown landscape beyond.

When they got to the car park, Saskia said 'This is us,' and pulled open the driver's door of a red pick-up truck.

'You drive?' asked Kier, surprised.

'Well, let's see, shall we?'

She revved the engine, put her arm over the back seat and released the clutch so that the truck spun backwards in a neat arc. Then she tapped the brakes, pushed it into first gear and accelerated out of the car park in a cloud of dust.

She turned to Kier and smiled.

'Yep,' she said, 'I guess I do.'

They rolled down the windows and Saskia took the coast road, gunning the engine as Kier gazed out past olive groves to the turquoise sea beyond.

'You still haven't told me where we're going,' he said.

'Stop worrying,' said Saskia, her hair whipping around her face in the breeze. 'You'll find out soon enough.'

They turned off on to a long straight road with vineyards on either side of them. After a few kilo-metres they came to a pair of thick wooden gates with purple-flowered bougainvillea cascading over the surrounding walls. Saskia pressed a button on the key fob and the gates swung open with an electronic hum, revealing a sweep of driveway bordered by green lawns. Small rainbows hovered between the sprinklers as droplets of water danced above damp grass. Kier could see steps at the end of the drive leading to a stone terrace and a large whitewashed villa.

'Wow,' he said as Saskia parked the truck next to a shiny black BMW. 'Someone's not short of a few quid.'

Saskia nodded. 'He worked hard for it. And he looks after his people too.'

Kier wondered who he was and who his people were, but guessed he would find out soon enough.

As they walked up the steps, two men appeared at the front door. They were similar in appearance: both heavily built with close-cropped hair and tanned faces. In spite of the heat, they wore the uniform loved by security guards the world over: sunglasses, white shirts and dark suits with a slight bulge under the left pocket, indicating the handgun concealed beneath.

'I feel like I'm in a film,' Kier whispered.

'You are,' said Saskia, pointing at the security camera on the wall. 'It's all right,' she told the two men. 'He's with me.'

The men nodded and stepped aside.

One of them asked, 'Are you Kier?'

'I am,' said Kier, taken aback.

'I'm sorry about your father. He was a good man. One of the best.'

'Thanks,' said Kier, wondering how it was that everyone seemed to know more about his father than he did.

As they entered the villa, he saw that the air-conditioned hallway was lined with potted palms, carefully positioned beneath spotlights which threw leafy shadows across the marble floor.

'You OK?' asked Saskia as they stopped outside a pair of thick oak doors.

Kier nodded. His father was dead and he was far from home in the company of strangers.

'I'm fine.'

'OK, well . . . good luck.'

Saskia twisted the handle and opened the door.

'I've brought him,' she said, gently pushing Kier forward. 'It's Kier – David's son.'

As Kier entered, the door closed behind him and he heard Saskia's footsteps echoing down the corridor.

The room was more modern than he had expected – open and light, with pine floors and shelves full of books. In the centre of the room, in front of a large picture window, was a solid oak desk with a computer and several neat piles of paper. But Kier's eye was immediately drawn to the man seated behind it. Kier guessed he must be in his early fifties: his hair was greying at the temples and a few lines were visible beneath the mahogany tan. But he had kept himself in good shape. Beneath the crisp white shirt was the short, stocky physique of a rugby player and the blue eyes that met Kier's were as hard and clear as diamonds. Kier imagined him in his younger days, hunched forward in a scrum, driving towards the line.

'Kier,' he said, standing up and smiling as if they had known each other all their lives. 'Welcome to the Retreat.' He offered his hand across the desk. 'Richard Jackson. I was a good friend of your father.'

Another one, thought Kier, shaking the man's hand.

'Please. Take a seat.'

Kier sat and watched as another dark suit walked past the window. Jackson, it seemed, was a man who liked protection.

'I imagine things must have been rather difficult for you recently.'

'You could say that.'

'Your father's death was a great loss to us all.'

Kier took a deep breath.

'Why do I get the feeling,' he asked, 'that everyone knows more about this than I do?'

Jackson shook his head. 'Not everyone. Only those involved.'

'Involved with *what*?'

Jackson rested his arms on the desk and fixed Kier with a cool stare.

'You must understand, Kier, that people's lives are at stake here.'

Kier stared right back.

'I think I understand that better than most.'

'I think you probably do.' Jackson opened a cream-coloured folder, glanced inside and closed it again. 'Tell me, how much do you know about your father?'

Kier shrugged.

'Not much. I know he was in the army before he joined the police. Then, after my mother died, he went to work for a property development firm. He was travelling around a lot, so I was sent to boarding school.'

Jackson nodded; this was obviously not news to him.

'The property business is mine and your father worked for me.' He waved his arm to indicate the room and the grounds beyond it. 'You're looking at a very rich man, Kier. I have properties all over the world.'

Kier wasn't sure why Jackson was telling him this, but he decided to try and steer the conversation back on track.

'So you knew my father?'

'We were in the Parachute Regiment together. When we left the army he joined the police force and I built up a business.' Jackson smiled. 'You know, I once offered your father ten times what they were paying him to come and work for me. But he wasn't interested in money. He was one of the good guys, you see. He wanted to make a difference.'

Kier nodded, remembering what his father had said to him after the tournament.

Find out what matters, that's the real secret.

'We kept in touch, you know. Birthdays, Christmas, that kind of thing. But then the world began to change. Suddenly it seemed that there were drug dealers on every street corner. People who wouldn't think twice about killing their own mothers if they could make something out of it.'

Jackson got up and walked to the window. Outside, a swimming pool sparkled in the sunlight.

'They killed my son, Kier. He was the same age as you when they got to him.'

'I'm sorry,' said Kier, not knowing what else to say.

Jackson shrugged.

'It's a tough world. But after that I couldn't stand it any more. I took my millions and came to live out here where the sun shines twelve hours a day and crime is virtually non-existent. I thought maybe I could find a way to be happy again.'

'And did you?'

'Oh, it was OK for a while. But the trouble was, I no longer had a reason to get up in the mornings. Then one night I got a phone call from your dad. He told me that while he was off duty, some guy had attacked him in the street and tried to take his wallet. Your dad fought back and next thing he knew, he was being arrested for assault.'

'Arrested?' Kier couldn't believe it. 'But I thought you said he was the one who got attacked?'

'Absolutely, but your dad was a fighter, remember. So the other guy was left with cuts and bruises, while your dad didn't have a scratch on him. I hired the best lawyer I could and he got off with a caution. But that was the end of his police career.'

'He lost his job?'

'Not exactly. But they made it pretty difficult for him after that, so he resigned. Just because he'd tried to do the right thing, he was left without a job and a young kid to bring up. And that's when I decided enough was enough.'

Kier looked at the sunlight shining on the bright lawn and realised that until this moment he had known almost nothing of his father. Now, as the truth began to unfold in front of him, he wanted to know everything.

'What happened?'

'Your father always wanted the best for you, Kier. But like me he was an idealist: he wanted to make the world a better place for you to grow up in. Which is why he agreed to work with me on my . . . other project. He couldn't look after you on his own, so I offered to pay for you to attend boarding school.'

Kier had often wondered how his father could afford the school fees. Now things were starting to make sense.

'What exactly was your other project?'

'I used contacts from my army days and others I have made since to create – oh, what shall we call it? – a kind of police force of my own.'

'A police force?'

'Yes. But a police force that hasn't had its teeth removed by a thousand rules and regulations. A police force that, to all intents and purposes, does not exist.'

'Why?'

'Times have changed, Kier. The old ways don't work any more and it's time for something harder, stronger. Something that still knows how to bite.'

'So how big is this . . . organisation?'

'Not huge. There are a handful of people on active service at any time.'

'And Saskia is one of them?'

'Correct.'

'How come?'

'Unfortunately her parents died when she was very young. I'd always said that if anything happened to them, I'd make sure she was well looked after. I arranged for her to receive a private education out here in Crete. But – as I expect you have already discovered – Saskia is a very single-minded young woman. When she became aware of some of the – how shall I put it? – *activities* that were taking place around the island, she was determined to be a part of them. I indulged her for a while, thinking she would soon lose interest. But it quickly became apparent that she had the potential to become a highly skilled operative. As has since been proved.'

'But isn't that dangerous?'

'Life is dangerous, Kier. One thing I've learned is, if you want to change things, you have to take risks.

And besides, no one made her do it. To tell the truth, it would have been impossible to stop her.'

'But even so – isn't she a bit young?'

'I don't think so. Interestingly enough, she was actually fourteen when she started. Which I happen to think is a very good age to begin.'

Kier frowned.

'Meaning?'

'Meaning that you might want to help us find the people who killed your father.'

Kier stared at him.

'Are you serious?'

'Oh, I'm deadly serious.'

'But what can I do?'

'A lot more than you think,' said Jackson. 'But we should talk about that later.' He rested his chin on the tips of his fingers and studied Kier for a few moments. 'You've had a difficult couple of days and all this must have come as quite a shock to you. I think what you need now is some time for reflection.'

Jackson pushed back his chair and got to his feet, signifying that the meeting was at an end.

'There's an old friend of mine who has a beautiful place not far from here. It's a simple, quiet place where you can gather your thoughts and begin to prepare yourself.'

As Kier closed the door and walked through the cool shadows of the hallway, he thought about what Jackson had said.

Prepare myself? Prepare myself for what?

'So what did he say?' asked Saskia.

Kier hung his arm out of the window as the truck gathered speed, feeling the breeze ripple through his fingers.

'He told me about your parents,' he said. 'I'm sorry.'

Saskia shrugged and kept her eyes on the road ahead.

'It was a long time ago.'

They passed an olive grove and Kier watched a few shabby goats wandering aimlessly across the blood-red earth. He looked at the trees in their neat, careful rows and wondered when some semblance of order would return to his own life.

'Did he ask you if you wanted to join?' said Saskia.

'Yeah, kind of. He wants me to help find the people who killed my father.'

'Ah.' Saskia nodded. 'That must be why he's sending you to Chiang.'

Up ahead, Kier saw the honey-coloured walls of an old monastery rising out of the dusty soil.

'Chiang?' he said. 'Who the hell is Chiang?'

EIGHT

Kier stood alone in the afternoon heat, watching Saskia drive away along the rough dirt track. When the dust had settled and he could no longer see her, he turned and walked up the steps of the monastery.

At the top of the steps was an archway which led through a cloistered area shaded by vines to an open courtyard. Kier could see a thin, sandy-coloured cat asleep in the shade of an old wheelbarrow and another lazily batting an olive stone around in the dust. At some time in the past, someone had taken the trouble to build several raised beds out of stone and, despite the dry heat, the beds were full of brightly coloured flowers. The only sound was the chirruping of cicadas in the olive groves.

'Hello?' he called. 'Is anyone around?'

The cat under the wheelbarrow raised its head, blinked and then went back to sleep again.

Kier crossed the courtyard and climbed another set of steps built into the far wall. They led to a covered stone balcony which encircled the perimeter of the courtyard. On one side of the balcony was a waist-high wall overlooking the courtyard. On the other side were four wooden doors, their pale blue paint faded and blistered by the sun. Kier rapped gently on the first door and, when there was no reply, twisted the handle and pushed it open. The room was small with a simple wooden desk in one corner and a straw mattress on the floor. Through the open window, Kier could see the sea sparkling in the distance.

Don't worry, Saskia had told him before driving away. *Everything will be fine.*

But everything wasn't fine. He was hot, tired and thirsty. And whoever he was supposed to be staying with was obviously not here.

'You are looking for someone, perhaps?'

Kier turned to see a small, bald man dressed in what appeared to be cotton pyjama bottoms and a baggy white T-shirt. It was hard to say how old he was but the skin on his face was crinkled and the colour of old pine. Kier guessed he had to be at least seventy, maybe older. He had a thin, bony frame which gave the impression that a light breeze might just blow him away.

'You scared me,' said Kier, taking a step backwards. 'I didn't hear you coming.'

'That is because you were not listening hard enough.'

Kier frowned, puzzled by this strange response.

'Look, Mr Jackson sent me over. I don't know if anyone told you, but I'm supposed to be staying here for a few days. I think I'm meant to be meeting someone called ... Chiang. Do you know him?'

The man bowed his head slightly. 'I am Chiang. And you are Kier, yes?'

'Yes,' said Kier, relieved. It wasn't much, maybe, but it was a start.

'You have had a long journey?'

'Yes.'

'And you are hot, I expect. Tired and thirsty too, no doubt.'

'As a matter of fact, I am.'

'Good. That is very good.'

Chiang motioned Kier forward with his hand. 'Come. Follow me.'

He turned and began to walk back towards the steps.

Kier stared after him and shook his head. 'Weird,' he said under his breath. But he followed Chiang down the steps and across the courtyard. To Kier's surprise, they left the monastery and began walking along a rough, dusty path.

'Where are we going?' asked Kier.

'For a walk,' said Chiang.

After a few minutes the path narrowed and they began to descend into a steep, rocky gorge. The sun was fierce and the sides of the gorge trapped the heat like an oven, so that Kier's clothes were soon soaked in sweat. He had a raging thirst and his whole body felt as if it might shrivel in the heat. What he had imagined would be a short, gentle stroll had turned into a tortuous, hour-long descent into a blast furnace. But ahead of him, Chiang seemed completely unaffected, continuing to maintain a steady, even pace.

Just when Kier was on the verge of giving up, the path twisted around to the left and he found himself standing in a sheltered cove. Sunlight reflected off white pebbles and he stared longingly at the blue water, desperate for something to cool his sunburnt skin.

'It is beautiful, yes?'

'Yes.' Kier blinked and wiped sweat from his brow. 'It is very beautiful.'

He took off his shoes and socks, then began removing his jeans and T-shirt. Chiang said nothing, watching him in silence until Kier stood dressed in just a pair of white boxer shorts.

'Come,' he said. 'We have some climbing to do.'

Kier could hardly believe what he was hearing. Didn't the guy ever get tired?

'Listen,' he suggested, trying to be reasonable. 'How about we just swim and cool off for a bit first?'

Chiang shook his head.

'No swimming now. Swimming later, perhaps.'

Kier was about to protest when he saw a look in Chiang's eyes that made him think better of it. Wearily he followed him across the beach, listening to the cool waves lap softly against the stones. After a while, the heat became almost unbearable. But Kier remained silent, gritting his teeth and pulling himself up after Chiang as he scaled the steep cliff. After they had been climbing for several minutes, Chiang suddenly swung himself sideways and led Kier across to a flat rock that jutted out over the sea.

'Come,' he said. 'Stand beside me.'

Kier stood next to him and looked down at the blue water below.

'Close your eyes,' said Chiang.

Kier did as he was told and felt the sun beating down on the top of his head.

'Now tell me how you feel.'

'Hot,' said Kier. 'Thirsty. Tired.'

'This is how you felt before we left,' said Chiang. 'How do you feel now?'

'Ten times worse,' replied Kier.

'Do you think it could get a hundred times worse?'

Kier felt the blood throbbing in his temples and began to suspect that Chiang was completely mad. He rubbed sweat from his eyelids and opened them again.

'If I stand here much longer, then yes.'

'You are angry, I think.'

Kier grunted.

'Do you know why you are angry?'

'Well, let's see. Maybe it's because I'm standing here in the sun, when all I want to do is go for a swim and sit in the shade with a cool drink.'

'You want these things very much?'

'Yeah.'

'What else do you want?'

'I want to wash. I want to get some sleep.'

'And?'

This was crazy. Kier screwed up his eyes and tried to think of an answer that would shut the old man up. His whole body burned and, as his head swam in the heat, he thought of rain falling and the sound of gunshots . . .

'I want to know who killed my father. I want to stop them from killing me. And I want my life to be normal again.'

Chiang nodded.

'These are good answers. Tell me. When you first followed me, did you believe I was going to fetch you a drink?'

'Yes.'

'And you were disappointed when I did not fetch you one?'

'Yes.'

'You wanted a swim when we arrived at the beach. Were you angry when I did not allow it?'

'I guess so.'

'You wanted something, but you did not get it. You expected something to happen, but something else happened instead. This is what life does to us, I think.'

'So why make it worse than it already is?' asked Kier irritably. 'Why bring me all the way out here just to tell me that?'

'Because this way, you will remember.'

'Remember what?' Kier was angry now. 'That I once went for a walk with a crazy man?'

Chiang smiled. 'Perhaps. But also that we should not let unexpected hardships remove us from the path. If we learn to be patient, to endure, then the things we seek will be sweeter in the end.'

'Great,' said Kier sarcastically. 'Can I swim now?'

'Of course,' said Chiang, 'and when you have

finished, there will be a cool drink waiting for you.'

Kier stood at the end of the rock and stared down at the blue water below. He paused, savouring the moments between desire and fulfilment. Then, stretching up his arms, he leapt into a graceful swallow dive, feeling the shock of cold water as he plunged beneath the surface and swam down to the smooth rocks at the bottom. Following the trail of silver bubbles to the surface, he looked up and saw that the rock above was empty.

Chiang was nowhere to be seen.

Kier floated on his back and wondered if his life could get any stranger. Staring up at the sky, he tasted salt water on his lips and thought about the cold drink Chiang had promised. But when he got back to the beach there was still no sign of the old man, so he lay on the hot stones and hoped he wouldn't be too long.

After five minutes, Kier was completely dry.

After ten minutes of getting hotter and thirstier, it occurred to him that Chiang wasn't coming back.

Angrily pulling on his clothes, he set off into the sweltering gorge again, passing the time by calling Chiang every rude name he could think of.

When he arrived back at the monastery it was silent and empty, just as before. But Kier was still angry, determined to find Chiang and ask him why he had not kept his promise.

Striding across the courtyard, he searched for signs of the old man. Finding none, he climbed the steps, only to discover that the door he had opened previously was now closed once more. He turned the handle and pushed it open, half-expecting to find Chiang seated at the desk or lying on the small mattress. But the room was empty and just as it had always been.

Except that, in the very centre of the stone floor, was a glass of cold water.

Kier smiled.

Chiang was crazy, no doubt about it.

All that strange talk about life and its hardships.

But as Kier slowly lifted the glass to his lips, he knew the old man had been right about one thing.

The water tasted sweeter than any he had ever tasted before.

NINE

He awoke to find the room in darkness. At first he was confused, until he remembered how he had lain on the mattress, thinking he would just close his eyes for a moment or two. Tiredness had obviously got the better of him and he had fallen asleep.

He felt rested, but he was still hot and his throat was dry. As he sat up, he noticed a fresh bottle of water had been placed next to his bed and, unscrewing the top, he drank from it greedily. A T-shirt and a pair of white cotton trousers had been left on the desk and Kier was glad to remove his jeans and replace them with the cooler, loose-fitting trousers. He pulled on the T-shirt, opened the door and wandered out on to the balcony.

In the courtyard below, Chiang was sitting cross-legged in the dust. Kier watched him for several minutes to see what he would do. But he remained perfectly still, his eyes closed and his hands resting in his lap like two sleeping birds.

Weird as ever, thought Kier. But the old man intrigued him. Kier guessed that if he hung around a while longer he'd probably find out more about what Jackson had planned for him. And if that meant wearing pyjamas for a few days and listening to Life According to Chiang, then he supposed he'd just have to put up with it.

Padding down the steps, he crossed the courtyard cautiously, not wanting to give the old man a heart attack. He had just decided to skirt around by the wall and approach from the front when, without moving from his position, Chiang said quietly, 'Are you rested?'

'Yes,' Kier replied, surprised to find Chiang aware of his presence. 'I slept very well.'

In one smooth, fluid movement, Chiang rose from the ground, turned and gestured towards an olive tree.

'Come then. Let us eat.'

Kier frowned. It had to be about three in the morning.

Beneath the olive tree, a small table had been set with wooden plates and bowls. In the centre was some bread and three small bowls filled with olives, honey and yoghurt. It felt strange to be sitting down for a meal at a time when he would normally be sleeping, but there was something oddly exciting about it too. The moon was bright, the sky was full of stars and although the sun was on the other side of the world, its warmth still rose silently from the stones.

Kier watched Chiang put yoghurt and honey into his bowl and then did the same, pouring the honey in neat circles before finally spooning the mixture into his mouth.

'It is good?' asked Chiang.

Whether it was something about the hour, or the things that had happened to him over the past couple of days, Kier couldn't say, but as the sweetness dissolved on his tongue it was as if he had broken through a hidden wall to touch and taste the world for the very first time.

'Yes,' he said. 'It's really good.'

Chiang tore off a hunk of bread and placed it on Kier's plate.

'Eat more. You will need your strength today, I think.'

Uh-oh, thought Kier, wondering what else Chiang had planned. But as the first rays of sunlight began to edge above the mountains, he realised that he was actually looking forward to finding out.

'Mr Jackson tells me you are a trained fighter,' said Chiang, leading Kier into a room overlooking the sea.

'Not really,' said Kier. 'I've done a bit.'

There was a vase of flowers on the window ledge, sharing the space with a shallow bowl and a water jug. In the centre of the room was a patterned carpet, its once bright colours faded over the years. Chiang walked into the middle and turned to face him.

'Tell me,' he said, 'about your last fight.'

Kier thought for a moment. 'Well, there was the fight on the train. But Saskia took care of that.'

'Then that was not your last fight.'

'OK. Well, before that, I got attacked by a man with a knife.'

Chiang's face brightened.

'Very good.'

Very good? thought Kier. *What was good about it?*

'And what happened?'

'I got rid of the knife. Then I ran away.'

'Show me.'

'How I got rid of the knife?'

'Yes.' Chiang raised his hand as if it held an imaginary weapon. 'Show me.'

Kier tensed his stomach muscles, trying not to laugh. He didn't want to appear rude, but it was ridiculous, this old man pretending to attack him.

'He didn't hold it like that.'

'Like this, perhaps?' Chiang lowered his hand and moved it forward in a stabbing motion.

'Yeah. Something like that.'

'And what did you do?'

Kier stepped forward and twisted slowly, moving his arm up until it touched Chiang's.

'No. Show me properly.'

'What?'

'You move like a snail in treacle. Show me how it really was.'

'Well, OK. But don't say I didn't warn you.'

As Chiang moved his arm forward once more, Kier twisted quickly and made a grab for his wrist, intending to lower him gently on to the carpet. But suddenly the space where Chiang's arm had been was empty and, before he knew what was happening, Kier hit the floor with a force that knocked all the wind out of him.

'Thank you for warning me,' said Chiang, bowing politely. 'But I think I am all right.'

Kier rested his head on his knees, waiting for his breath to come back.

'Perhaps you would like to show me again?' asked Chiang.

Kier raised his head and looked at the old man. He was standing in exactly the same spot, arms hanging loosely by his sides. He could have been waiting in line to collect his pension.

But appearances, it seemed, were deceptive.

Kier got to his feet and regarded Chiang warily. The guy was obviously tougher than he looked. This time, Kier decided, he wouldn't mess about. This time, he would show him what he could really do.

'OK,' he said. 'Ready when you are.'

He waited for Chiang to step forward, to move his arm within range. Then – as the arm reached its full extension – he ducked beneath it and thrust his fist upwards, aiming for the soft flesh and the cluster of nerve endings on the underside of the wrist. It was a move he had practised many times; he knew from experience that it would hurt and unbalance his opponent, opening up the body enough for him to step in and take his pick of targets. But instead of his fist hitting the old man's wrist as expected, it continued on its upward path through empty air. Then something brushed against the side of his head, his temple stung with a strange heat and suddenly the world exploded and went black.

Kier opened his eyes to find himself staring at the ceiling, trying to remember what his name was. Then an old man in a baggy T-shirt leaned over him and the memories began swimming back through a thick grey fog. Slowly, he sat up and touched his head, which felt numb, as if it was encased in concrete.

The old man crouched in front of him and placed his hands on either side of Kier's head. Then, with one quick movement, he flicked his thumbs across Kier's temples and the numbness melted away like snow in springtime.

'Better?'

Kier nodded.

'I think so.'

'You must breathe deeply, like this.' Chiang placed a hand on his chest and breathed slowly, in, out, in case Kier had forgotten how. Kier copied the rhythm of his breathing and after a minute or two his mind was clear again.

'What happened?' he asked.

'You were showing me how to disarm a man with a knife.'

Kier nodded. 'How did I do?'

'Not so good. But lucky for you I never kill my students.' Chiang crossed his legs and rested his hands in his lap. 'If I kill them, they do not learn.'

'But I don't get it,' said Kier. 'I've been doing that move for years and it's never failed before.'

'Then that is why it fails now.'

'I don't understand.'

'You look at me and experience tells you I am weak. You think the past is a reliable guide to the future. This is not so.'

'But it worked on the guy with the knife.'

'Of course, just as a knife will cut through butter. But use it to cut through stone and things will be different, I think.'

'So you're saying my karate is useless?'

'No. But karate is a blunt instrument, carried by many. Far better to have something that is part of you. Something which can change to suit the moment. You see?'

'Sort of,' said Kier.

'Good.'

Chiang stood up and bowed his head.

'Then let us begin.'

TEN

'Someone is about to attack you,' warned Chiang. 'Show me your defence.'

Kier shifted two-thirds of his weight on to his back foot and pointed the other foot towards Chiang. Then he held his left palm face outwards and drew his right fist back against his hip.

'No,' said Chiang. 'No, no, no, no, *no*.'

'What?'

'I look at you and straight away I know what you are going to do. You might as well send me a postcard.'

'How can you possibly know?' Kier's fist tightened with irritation. 'I could be about to do one of a thousand things.'

'All right,' said Chiang, 'then do them.'

Kier took a deep breath, held it beneath his diaphragm and focused on Chiang's hands, looking for the slightest flicker of movement. He was ready this time. He would wait until the—

'Ow! Ahhh . . . *Uhnnnnff!*'

'You see?' said Chiang, as Kier lifted his face from the carpet. 'You are too tense, too rigid, too *angry*. You must learn to relax.'

Relax? thought Kier. *How can I relax when you keep throwing me on the floor?*

'You must stand naturally,' Chiang told him when he was on his feet again. 'This way you are a blank page and there is nothing for anyone to read. No one knows what you are going to do.'

'Including me,' said Kier.

'Including you,' agreed Chiang.

Kier frowned.

'So how's that going to help?'

'Because if you do not know, then your opponent will be unable to guess. You will retain the element of surprise.'

Kier stared at Chiang, trying to make sense of what he said. But it was no good. The man talked in riddles.

'Then how will I know what to do?'

'You must learn to separate thought from action. You must train your body so that it can react to each new situation as it arises.'

Chiang walked over to the window ledge and filled the shallow bowl with water from the jug. He took a red flower and a yellow flower from the vase, then returned with the bowl and placed it carefully on the floor between them. When Kier raised his eyebrows, Chiang simply inclined his head in the direction of the bowl and together they watched the water settle back into stillness.

'What do you see?' asked Chiang.

'I see a bowl of water.'

'And what do you notice about it?'

'Umm, the bowl is white.'

'Yes.'

'It's made from clay.'

'Yes.'

Kier was confused. What else was he supposed to say?

'Tell me about the water.'

'It's clear.'

'Yes.'

'It's not moving. The water is still.'

'Was it moving before?'

'Yes, when you carried it.'

'But there is no movement now?'

Kier stared at the water and saw only his reflection in its smooth surface.

'No. The water is still.'

With lightning speed Chiang slapped his hand into the bowl, sending droplets of water flying in all directions. Some fell on to the carpet, some on to

Kier's cotton trousers and some on to the stones. Kier's heart beat faster at this unexpected movement, but he remained silent as Chiang picked up the red flower and handed it to him.

'The day is warm and the water will soon be gone,' he said. 'You must move quickly and place a petal on every droplet you see.'

Kier was about to ask why when he realised there was no point. He was already becoming familiar with Chiang's strange way of talking and knew it was best just to get on with it. Moving carefully, he searched for the dark spots where the water had landed and placed a red petal on each one. When he sat down again, he saw that there were still some petals left, so he tore them off and pressed them to the spots where the water had fallen on to his knees. Then he put the flower stalk to one side and stared at the patterns he had made, the petals dancing like embers from a fire.

Chiang fetched the jug of water, refilled the bowl and waited for the water to settle. Then he nodded in Kier's direction.

'Now you.'

Kier raised his hand and slapped the water just as Chiang had done. Without a word, Chiang picked up the yellow flower and began pulling off its petals, placing them on the spots where the water had fallen.

'What do you see?' he asked when he was sitting opposite Kier once more.

'I see a new pattern.'

'Is it different from before?'

Kier looked at the sprinkling of yellow petals and saw how some had fallen in the gaps between the red petals, while others had fallen upon them or beyond.

'Some parts are the same. But mostly it's different.'

'So you think the water is alive?'

'No.'

'Then how does it know to do something different each time it is slapped?'

'It doesn't know. It just does it.'

'It just does it?'

'Yes.'

'I see. But you agree that it does it differently each time?'

'I guess so.'

Kier was really confused now. He didn't have the faintest idea what Chiang was getting at. But then he supposed that was nothing new.

'So tell me. What is happening?'

Kier stared at the random pattern of red and yellow petals, trying to make sense of it.

'Maybe there was something different about the

way we hit the water,' he suggested. 'Perhaps I hit it harder, or softer, or at slightly more of an angle.'

'And if you were to hit it again? Would you be able to hit it in the same way as before?'

'No.'

'So the water does not have to think. It has only stillness. But the way we behave towards it changes the way it reacts. Do you see?'

Kier nodded.

'I think I'm starting to.'

'You must become like the water. The lessons you learn must dissolve in your blood until they are a part of you. Then you must hold them inside until the time comes for the world to break your stillness. When this happens, you will no longer need to ask the question "What shall I do?" because the answer will already be in your blood and in your bones.'

Kier looked at the petals and the water, and knew something was changing inside him. He felt the pulse of his blood and the warmth of his feet against the stones.

'Teach me more,' he said. 'Teach me everything you know.'

The next few weeks were the hardest of Kier's life, but at least he was beginning to understand what Jackson had meant by 'preparing himself'. The men who had murdered his father were professional, cold-blooded killers and if Jackson was serious about Kier looking for them, then Kier was going to need all the help he could get.

At first, Chiang would wake him at dawn and Kier would follow the old man in silence down to the courtyard, where breakfast would be set beneath the branches of the old olive tree. But after a while his body clock began to change and he would find himself standing alone in the courtyard, looking up at the moon. When that happened, he would walk quietly to the little storeroom, take out the yoghurt, bread and olives and set the table for breakfast. Then he would sit cross-legged in the shadows, practising his stillness and waiting for Chiang to awake. Although Chiang never said anything, Kier guessed by the gentle tilt of his head as he sat down at the table that he was pleased. After that, he always tried to be up first. There was something about looking after the old man that gave him a quiet satisfaction, helping him to fill the empty spaces inside.

One of the first things Chiang had said was, *You were not listening hard enough*, and Kier soon discovered this was something of a theme with him. *You were not listening hard enough, you were not looking hard enough, you were not feeling hard enough . . .*

Nothing was ever enough, and however hard Kier pushed himself, Chiang always pushed him harder.

'It is not enough to listen with your ears,' he said one day. 'You must also listen with your skin.'

Listen with your skin?

Kier was used to Chiang's strange pronouncements, but this was the weirdest so far.

Chiang made him take off his shirt and stood him a couple of metres in front of the storeroom door. Then he handed him two small twists of yellow rag.

'What are these for?' Kier asked.

'Put them in your ears,' said Chiang. 'Then face the other way and tell me when the door behind you opens.'

'Yeah, because that's useful,' said Kier. His muscles ached and he felt as if he hadn't slept in days. 'I'm really going to need that in my life.'

For the first time he noticed a flicker of anger in Chiang's eyes. It wasn't much – a brief shadow on a summer's day – but Kier saw it nonetheless.

'You think I do this for my own amusement?'

Muttering something under his breath about it certainly not being for *his* amusement, Kier stuffed the rags in his ears and turned away. He tried to feel the slight change in pressure on his skin that Chiang had told him would be there when the door

76

opened. But his heart wasn't in it and he kept getting it wrong. After the fifteenth or sixteenth failed attempt, Chiang crept up and slapped him sharply on the neck.

'Ow!' shouted Kier, outraged at this unexpected assault.

Pulling the rags from his ears, he stomped up the stairs to his room and slammed the door behind him.

For the rest of the day he lay on his mattress and fumed, calling Chiang every name under the sun. He kept expecting Chiang to appear at the door in that silent, spooky way he had, ready to chastise him for failing to learn his lessons properly. But when, after several hours, Chiang didn't appear, Kier's anger began to fade and tiredness overtook him.

When he awoke, the room was bathed in moonlight and Chiang was standing in the doorway, holding what appeared to be a piece of a cactus plant. It was shaped like a mouse's ear, sharp spines protecting its soft flesh and small spheres of orange-red fruit sprouting from its top edge. Kier had seen them growing in the courtyard and by the side of the road.

'Do you think I am too hard on you?' Chiang asked, sitting cross-legged in the middle of the floor.

Kier sat up and rubbed his eyes.

'I don't know. Sometimes, maybe.'

Chiang held up the cactus.

'You know what this is?'

Kier looked at it warily, worried that Chiang might suddenly whack him with it.

'It's a cactus.'

'Yes, a prickly pear. It grows in deserts, dry scrubland, places where most things would be unable to survive. And yet it does survive. Look.'

Kier leaned forward and saw that, between the sharp thorns, there were needle-fine hairs ready to prick and pierce the skin of the unwary.

'It has evolved to protect itself from the things that would seek to destroy it.'

'Right,' said Kier, wondering why Chiang had turned up in the middle of the night to tell him this.

'Your life has changed, I think. From now on there will be many things that will tear at your flesh and attempt to devour you. So, like the cactus, your defences must be strong. Growing them will be painful. But behind them, the goodness will remain.'

Chiang took a small knife from his pocket and began expertly removing the cactus spikes before cutting one of the red fruits from the top. He held it in his palm and sliced down its middle. As the fruit fell into two halves, Kier was surprised to see that inside was soft purple flesh, juicy and studded with small black seeds.

'Here,' said Chiang, handing him a piece.

Kier put the fruit in his mouth and felt its sweetness dissolve on his tongue, the sugary juice overflowing and dribbling down his chin.

'Now do you understand?' asked Chiang.

Kier nodded, wiping the juice away with his fingers. 'I understand.'

'Good,' said Chiang. 'Then you must take strength from this sweetness, for there is still much work to be done.'

Kier looked at the moon on the water and bowed his head.

'I am ready,' he said.

ELEVEN

'How was it?' asked Saskia as Kier climbed into the truck beside her.

'It was . . . interesting,' said Kier.

It had been nearly six weeks since Saskia had dropped him off at the monastery, six weeks of increasingly strange lessons involving – among other things – running up walls, dodging logs on ropes and standing silently in the darkness, trying to detect the exact moment when the hungry mosquitoes would land. But it was only now that he realised how much he had changed, and not just physically. It was true that every gram of excess fat had fallen away from his body and his jeans felt strangely constricting, despite the fact that they now hung loosely around his hips. But it was more than that. He felt calmer, less troubled, as if he had been pulled from a stormy sea and washed on to the sands of a foreign shore.

'It's a pretty intense few weeks, huh?'

'You've been there too?'

Saskia grinned.

'Oh yeah. Everyone on the programme gets to spend some quality time with Chiang.'

'So what happens now? Will Jackson tell me what he's got planned?'

'Maybe. But it won't be before you've had some driving lessons and a couple of days with a firearms instructor.'

'Driving lessons?' said Kier, feeling his earlier calm beginning to desert him. 'Firearms instructor?'

'Don't worry,' said Saskia. 'It'll be fun.'

The next few days were spent at an underground shooting range in the company of a short, red-haired American named Baz. Baz was built like a bulldog and wore the kind of pained expression that suggested someone had flattened his kennel and taken his bone away.

'This here's a pump-action shotgun,' he told Kier, after showing him how to take an AK-47 rifle apart and put it back together again. He aimed it at the cardboard soldier at the end of the range and blasted two quick shots into it. 'See? Find yourself on the wrong end of it and it'll punch a hole the size of a fist in your chest.'

'I know,' said Kier. 'I remember.'

'Listen, kid,' said Baz. 'I heard about what happened, OK? But that's all the more reason why you need to know about this stuff.'

'But I don't want to kill anyone,' said Kier.

'You don't have to. But you do have to learn how not to be killed. And the more you know about these things, the easier that's going to be. OK?'

'OK,' said Kier. After the calm of the monastery, the crackle of gunfire and smell of smoke came as something of a shock. But within a short time he enjoyed the discipline of learning something new and soon became adept at handling a range of weapons, from the small 9mm Browning pistol to the more substantial Heckler & Koch sub-machine gun.

'You're a pretty good shot,' said Baz after Kier had put a cluster of bullets into a target twenty-five metres away. 'To tell you the truth, it's a long time since I saw anyone with such a steady arm.'

Kier smiled as he thought of the hours he'd spent with Chiang learning to control his breathing and his heartbeat, learning to become still like the water.

He knew the old man would have appreciated that.

After two days spent underground in the artificial

glare of fluorescent lights, Kier was glad to be out in the fresh air again.

'What you have to remember,' said his instructor, Frankie, as they sat in a green Land Cruiser looking out over a patch of dry scrubland, 'is that all cars are pretty much the same.'

Kier recognised him as one of the men in suits from Jackson's villa, but he definitely seemed more at home in shorts and a T-shirt. Although he was a good twenty years older than Kier, Frankie treated him like an equal and seemed determined that they should have a good time.

'Mr Jackson calls this a training session,' he said. 'I call it a chance to mess around in someone else's motor and get paid for it. You ready?'

Kier grinned.

'Oh yeah,' he said. 'I'm ready.'

Frankie floored the accelerator, spinning the tyres, and Kier was thrown back hard against his seat as they shot across the dry red earth.

'Woo-hoo!' cried Frankie, continuing to acceler-ate until, just as Kier felt certain they would crash, he pulled on the handbrake and the back end slewed sideways in a cloud of dust. Releasing the handbrake, Frankie stamped on the accelerator again and the car rocketed back in the direction they had come.

'How are you liking it so far?' he yelled above the howl of the engine.

'I'm loving it,' Kier shouted back as Frankie sent the car into a side skid around a large outcrop of rock, 'but if you carry on like this I'm going to have to change my trousers.'

Swinging the car around, Frankie nudged the gearstick into neutral and brought them smoothly to a halt.

'Right,' he said. 'Fancy a go?'

They swapped places and Kier adjusted the seat so his feet could reach the pedals.

'Ever driven before?'

Kier shook his head. 'Only a friend's motorbike. And that was in a field.'

'OK, no problem. We'll start with the basics and move on to handbrake turns later. See that pedal on the right?'

'Yep.'

'That's the accelerator or, as I like to call it, the fun pedal. Step on that and you're going places. But do it for too long and you could be in all kinds of trouble. Which is why you also need the one next to it.'

'The brake?'

'Very good. But – ah-ah – don't put your left foot on it – only ever use your right.'

'I thought my right foot was for the accelerator?'

'It is, but you don't want to be accelerating and braking at the same time, so always use the same foot for both. Your left foot is for the clutch pedal, which – surprise, surprise – is the one on the left.'

'Is that for changing gear?'

'Yeah, same as on a motorbike. When you want to change gear, just ease off the accelerator, push the clutch in and slot the gearstick up a notch. Then it's back on the accelerator again. Unless you're slowing down of course. And when you stop, just make sure you put the gearstick in neutral again. Like this.' Frankie waggled the gearstick to show it was in the central position between the gears. 'Got it?'

'I think so.'

'Ready to give it a go?'

'Definitely.'

Kier checked the gears were in neutral and then turned the ignition key. The engine rumbled into life and, as he depressed the accelerator pedal slightly, there was a deep, throaty roar from the exhaust.

'Feels good, don't it?' said Frankie. 'OK. Clutch in.'

Kier pushed the clutch down with his left foot.

'Right. Soon as you're ready, let it up again slowly

and increase your revs with the accelerator at the same time.'

'Now?' asked Kier.

'Whenever you like,' said Frankie.

Kier let the clutch out and the car jolted forward, then stalled.

'Try letting it out a bit more slowly,' said Frankie.

This time the car juddered and bounced forward a few metres before coming to rest.

Frankie grinned. 'We call that kangaroo petrol,' he said. 'It happens when you haven't quite got the accelerator sorted out. But you'll get it in the end. Just takes practice, that's all.'

After ten minutes of stopping and starting, Kier pulled away smoothly for the first time and Frankie cheered, leaned over and banged the horn.

'You'll win the Grand Prix yet!' he shouted.

Then he made Kier stop and do it all over again. An hour later, Kier was confidently changing up and down through the gears, practising emergency stops and steering the car around a series of stones that Frankie had laid out as an obstacle course. When, at the third time of trying, Kier had successfully reversed back around the course, Frankie patted him on the back.

'Time for a break,' he said, glancing at his watch. 'Let's take her down the road to the beach.'

'You want me to drive?' asked Kier.

'Yeah, why not? You've got it sussed, I reckon. And the roads are pretty quiet round here, so it shouldn't be a problem. Just make sure you look in your mirror before you indicate. Oh, and try not to kill anyone.'

After the rough terrain they had been driving on, the road felt smooth beneath the wheels. Kier quickly learned to judge his position by looking straight ahead rather than keeping his eyes glued to the tarmac in front of the bonnet.

'Best taxi driver in the whole of Crete,' said Frankie, leaning back and putting his hands behind his head. 'And the cheapest too.'

They stopped at a small sandy cove and ate lunch at a wooden beach bar in the shade of a tamarisk tree.

'Chicken souvlaki,' said Frankie, watching Kier slide chunks of meat from the end of his skewer. 'Makes a change from Chiang's menu, eh?'

'Sure does.' Kier popped a chunk into his mouth, savouring the taste of herbs and warm olive oil. 'You've spent time with him too?'

Frankie nodded. 'All part of the programme. Jackson met Chiang back in the 80s, when he was learning martial arts in Tibet. When the Chinese threatened to arrest Chiang for helping the West,

Jackson brought him back here.' Frankie wiped his plate with some bread and took a sip of beer. 'Chiang's quite a guy all right. But I couldn't live like he does. No way.'

'On your own, you mean?'

'No.' Frankie winked and lifted his glass. 'Without chips and an ice-cold beer.'

Kier smiled and watched the waves lapping at the shore. England suddenly seemed far away and long ago; like a different life.

'So what about me, Frankie? Where do I fit into all of this?'

'Well, you've still got plenty of driving to do before I'm done with you. But I guess you'll be finding out pretty soon after that.'

Frankie downed his beer, placed a twenty-euro note beneath his glass and winked.

'So make the most of that souvlaki. It might be a while before you see any more of it.'

TWELVE

When Kier arrived at the villa Jackson was sitting on the lawn beneath a large cream-coloured sunshade, sipping tea from a china cup.

'You look different,' he said by way of a greeting. As Kier joined him at the expensive hardwood table, Jackson clenched his fist and held it up for emphasis. 'Sharper. More toned.'

'More prepared?'

'Quite.' Jackson poured another cup of tea and handed it to Kier. 'So now perhaps we should finish our conversation. Do you recall it?'

Kier took a sip of tea and watched a plane scratch vapour trails across the sky. 'You wanted me to help you find the people who killed my father.'

Jackson nodded. 'Your father was trying to infiltrate a gang of drug dealers when he died and we're pretty sure they're the ones who killed him.'

'You know who they are?'

'Not exactly. But thanks to your father's work we

know they're part of a London-based operation, concentrated in an area south of the river. They're dumping thousands of pounds' worth of cocaine on the streets every day of the week.'

'So why aren't the police dealing with them?'

'Who knows? Maybe they can't find where the stuff's coming from. Maybe they've got too many forms to fill in. But that's where you come in.'

'Me?' Kier frowned. 'What can I do?'

'You can be invisible. Our biggest problem is that the gang knows about us. They caught one of our operatives trying to infiltrate their organisation and forced him to tell them everything he knew. Then they threw him off a cliff. It wasn't good.'

'You're not making this sound very appealing.'

'It'll be different this time, Kier. We've learned from our mistakes and we need someone with no history. Someone like you.'

'But they saw me at the hospital.'

'Close up?'

'No.'

'Then trust me, they won't remember you. They only went after you because you happened to be there.'

Kier realised Jackson was right. The reason they'd tracked him down was simply that they knew his father's address.

'OK. So what do you want me to do?'

'Just before he was killed, your father sent back some information about a planned bank robbery. Latest intelligence says it's due to take place in three days' time. We just need you to stay out of sight and take a few photos of the suspects.'

'That's it?'

'For now, yes.'

Jackson opened a white A4 envelope and handed Kier a grainy black and white photograph. It showed a wiry man of about fifty in a dark suit and tie, the angular face, short haircut and neatly trimmed moustache giving the impression of someone who had led a disciplined life. An ex-soldier perhaps. Kier studied it for a while before placing it back on the table.

'Who is it?'

'We don't know. But it was one of the last photographs your dad took, so there's a strong chance he's involved in some way. If he shows up when it all kicks off, I want you to get some pictures and follow him. Forget about the others. I want to know who this man is. He's our number one priority.'

Kier frowned. 'OK. So I sit outside a bank, take a few photos and follow this guy if he shows up. No problem. But if that's all you want me to do, what was the point of all that training?'

'This is only the beginning,' said Jackson, pouring another cup of tea and sliding it across the table. 'Your training is for what comes afterwards. And of course you won't be working alone. Another of our operatives flew out there today. Says she's very much looking forward to working with you.'

As Jackson leaned across the table and offered Kier his hand, Kier imagined Saskia sailing through passport control and disappearing into the crowd.

'Welcome aboard, Kier.'

'Thanks,' said Kier, shaking his hand. 'I think.'

Later, as he packed his new leather holdall with the neat little phone-camera and selection of crisp new clothes that had been left out for him, he felt a tingle of excitement.

He was going back to London.

He was going to see Saskia and track down the people who had turned his life upside down.

But this time things would be different.

This time he would be ready for them.

THIRTEEN

Kier sat outside the cafe off Baker Street and watched the steam rise from his cappuccino. It was already mid-August and people were out in shorts and T-shirts, eating ice creams and trying not to think about the jobs and offices they would soon be going back to.

He watched the two men walk by on the other side of the street, held the phone-camera to his eye and used the powerful zoom function to take a few quick shots. Then he swung it nonchalantly forty-five degrees and took a couple more of some pigeons on a rooftop. To anyone watching, he would just be some tourist taking holiday snaps with his phone.

'Excuse me?' Kier held up a finger at the waitress who was wiping down the table next to him. 'Could I get a blueberry muffin here?'

'Sure,' she said. 'Won't be a second.'

Kier took a sip of coffee and imagined Saskia

stepping off a tube somewhere, walking through the shadows into the light. Not looking directly at anyone, seemingly lost in her own little world. But he knew she would be noticing everything, storing it away in case she needed it.

'Here you go. One blueberry muffin.'

The waitress smiled, put it down on the table and placed the bill underneath the plate. Kier noticed that she was pretty and reminded himself to focus. Picking up the muffin, he put a five-pound note in its place.

'Thanks. Keep the change.'

Ten minutes later the two men were still there, walking nervously up and down. But there was no sign of the man in the photograph.

Kier took a couple more pictures and then turned to see the waitress, who had now finished her shift, walk across the road and turn left towards the bank.

'Oh no,' whispered Kier under his breath. 'Don't do that. Just keep walking.'

The waitress stopped outside the bank. Then she opened the door and went in.

Kier stood up and saw one of the men peer through the bank window, shielding his face against the sun. As the other one walked back to join him, Kier reminded himself that he didn't even know the girl. *Don't get involved*, he told himself. But then the two men ran into the bank and suddenly Kier was dodging through traffic, standing outside and scanning the street for signs of police activity.

He breathed deeply, not because he was nervous, but because that was the way he had been taught. Get the oxygen to the muscles, keep the heart rate steady and don't let the adrenalin fire until the last moment.

Three minutes tops, he thought. *Three minutes and I'm out of there.*

He opened the door a fraction and slipped through, pressing himself against the wall and letting the information wash over him. The men had already squirted the security cameras with shaving foam, which was good news. They were both holding shotguns, one wearing a black bala-clava and the other with a pair of tights pulled over his head. The waitress lay on the floor with six other people and a woman who was screaming. The smell of cordite filled the air and chunks of plaster lay on the carpet where one of the men had already fired his shotgun into the ceiling.

Nervous, thought Kier. *Probably their first time.*

'Give me the money!' Balaclava was yelling. 'Give me the money now!'

Tights turned and pointed his shotgun at the people on the floor.

'Stay down!' he screamed at a man in a grey suit who had made the mistake of looking up. 'Kiss the carpet or I'll blow your head off!'

Kier concentrated on keeping perfectly still while he considered his next move. The men were so fired up they hadn't even noticed him yet, but he knew that any sudden movement could spook them into shooting up the place. Probably easier to deal with them than to try and move the girl. He thought back to the nights when Chiang had made him stand motionless, hour after hour, waiting for the hungry mosquitoes to settle.

It is the strength of their desire that makes them steal from you. So the strength of your desire to stop them must be stronger.

It had taken six weeks. Six weeks of enduring bites and Chiang saying, *No*, listen with your skin. But then, finally, he had understood. He had felt every touch, every cool whisper against the heat of his skin, and his hands moved lightning-fast, fingers plucking the insects away at the moment of landing, sometimes even before. After three hours he didn't have a single bite.

The strength of your desire to stop them must be stronger . . .

'I said give me the money!'

Kier looked at the white-faced woman behind the

counter and saw that she was brave, because brave meant being scared and still doing what you had to do. He saw how her left shoulder dipped just a couple of millimetres, hardly noticeable unless you were looking for it, but enough to let her press the silent alarm beneath the counter.

The man placed the shotgun barrel against the glass.

'I won't tell you again,' he said.

'This glass is bulletproof,' she said. She tried to speak calmly, but her voice was shaking. 'You do know that, don't you?'

The man moved the barrel of his gun around until it was pointing at the man in the grey suit.

'How about him?' he asked. 'Is he bulletproof too?'

As the man covered his face, the cashier's lower lip trembled.

'I'll get it for you,' she said. 'But don't hurt him, OK? Just don't hurt him.'

'You!' Balaclava shouted at the other cashier. 'Go and help her! Now!'

As both cashiers made their way into the back room, Tights began pulling black bin bags from his pocket and Kier decided it was time to make his move.

'Hi,' he said, taking three steps forward. 'Are you guys making a film or something?'

The man's head jerked up in surprise and Kier saw how his nose was squashed out of shape by the tights, making his face look as though it had been moulded out of Plasticine.

'Get on the floor!' the man yelled.

'Hey,' said Kier, 'that's really good. Can I have your autograph?'

As the man pulled back the mechanism of the pump-action shotgun, Kier heard the cartridge thump into the chamber and cursed himself for not noticing that it wasn't already loaded. But then he saw the way the man's hands were shaking and guessed he probably shouldn't spend too much time thinking about it.

'I won't tell you again. On the floor!'

'OK, OK.' Kier held up his hands and smiled apologetically. 'No need to get upset.'

But the man was getting very upset, and Balaclava was turning round to see what the fuss was about.

Time to begin.

Still smiling, Kier transferred his weight to the balls of his feet, shifting his centre of gravity until his legs buckled at the knee. At the same time he spread his fingers slightly, hands a shoulder width apart as he moved towards the floor. All this in around one-tenth of a second. When he was at roughly a forty-five-degree angle to the ground he allowed himself a final glance to check the man's exact position, then took all the tension out of his muscles and let gravity do the rest. In the split second before he hit the floor he pushed back with the tips of his toes, ducked his head down and pressed his hands into the carpet. The resulting momentum carried him into a brief handstand before flicking him forward so that the soles of his feet landed hard and square in the centre of the man's chest. As the man went down, Balaclava raised his shotgun and Kier brought the heel of his palm up under his chin so that he crashed back into a table, flipping it sideways and sending leaflets fluttering through the air. The gun skidded across the carpet and Kier flicked it up with his foot, catching it and aiming the barrel at Tights, who was reaching for the other shotgun.

'I wouldn't if I were you,' he said.

But Tights wasn't listening, so when he brought the gun up with his finger curled around the trigger, Kier took aim and blew it out of his hands. As fragments of wood and metal pinged off the walls, Kier reloaded and spun around to face Balaclava, who was crawling across the carpet towards him.

'What was it again?' he asked. 'Oh yeah, that's right.'

He smiled and pointed the shotgun at him.

'Kiss the carpet.'

As the man lay down, Kier glanced around and decided that things weren't looking good. He'd put two armed robbers on the floor in less than a minute and he hadn't even broken sweat. Not quite the low-key observation Jackson had in mind.

Time I was gone, he thought.

He had just decided to slide the shotgun through the door handles on his way out when his phone rang. As he pulled it out to answer it and saw Saskia's name flash up on the display, the doors of the bank flew open and he was faced with three armed policemen, all aiming their guns at him.

'Armed police!' one of them shouted. 'Drop your weapon!'

Instead, Kier dropped the phone, lowered the barrel of the shotgun and pulled the trigger. As the phone exploded into a thousand pieces he dropped to the floor and lay still, waiting patiently for the three policemen to jump on his back with their heavy boots on and cuff him.

Which, three seconds later, is exactly what they did.

FOURTEEN

When Kier arrived at the police station the two bank robbers were already there, swearing and struggling with their handcuffs, which made lifting the driver's car keys a whole lot easier. As Kier palmed them into his pocket, he watched the arresting officer tap a code into the security lock and then he was ushered down a corridor into an interview room. The room was empty apart from a table and two plastic chairs.

'Have a seat,' said the police officer.

Kier thought about dropping him right there and then, but in the end he decided against it. After all, the guy was only doing his job. He walked around to the far side of the table, pulled out the chair and sat down.

'So, introductions. My name is Police Constable Doyle. Do you want to tell me yours?'

'It's Richard. Richard Smith.'

'Address?'

'Er, 5 Station Road.'

'Whereabouts?'

Kier thought about the names he had seen on the tube map.

'Finchley.'

Doyle looked at him.

'Is that true?'

'You can check it if you like.'

'Oh, I will.'

Go on then, thought Kier. But Doyle stayed where he was and wrote *Richard Smith, 5 Station Road* in his notebook. Kier wondered idly if such a place existed.

'So. Do you want to tell me what you were doing in the bank?'

Kier shrugged.

'I was walking past and I heard a bang, so I went in to see what was going on. You know. Just curious.'

'OK. So how do you explain the fact that, when officers arrived at the scene, they found you standing in the middle of the bank holding a shotgun?'

Kier turned his hand over and studied his fingernails.

'I can understand how that must look.'

'I'm sure you can. Particularly as you then went on to fire it.'

'Accidentally.'

'That's not the way I heard it.'

'No? How did you hear it?'

'I heard you dropped your phone and fired at it deliberately.' Doyle shook his head. 'You realise you were seconds away from getting killed?'

'Wouldn't be the first time,' said Kier, and then immediately wished he hadn't. Chiang was right. He really did have to learn the value of silence.

'What do you mean?'

'Nothing.'

'You're a part of this gang, aren't you?'

'No.'

'That's what you meant, isn't it?'

'No.'

'Come on, Richard, stop playing games with me. It will be easier for everyone concerned if you just start telling the truth. What was your role in all of this? Were you the lookout?'

'Like I said, I was just walking past.'

'We have witnesses, you know.'

Kier closed his eyes and revisited the moment when he had first made his move. Everyone had been face down on the carpet, except for the cashiers collecting the money out back. The guy was definitely bluffing. No one would have seen what had happened.

'So go ahead and ask them. I'm sure they'll tell you the same thing.'

'Then how do you explain the fact that you were holding the gun when the officers arrived?'

'I can't.'

'OK,' said Doyle, putting his notebook aside for a moment. 'You know what I think, Richard? I think that you're not like those other two out there. The truth is, I can't figure you out. You seem like a bright kid who's somehow got mixed up in all this. But the problem is, you're holding something back from me and I don't know what it is. And unless you tell me, I'm not going to be able to help you.'

Just for a moment, Kier was caught off guard by this unexpected kindness. He could tell that Doyle was being sincere, that he genuinely wanted to throw Kier some kind of lifeline. But there was no way Kier was going to take it, so he stayed silent.

Doyle sighed.

'Listen, Chief Superintendent Tyler is on his way over here and he doesn't see things the way I do. Believe me, the only things he's interested in are his crime figures. He's not a man you want to mess with. So here's the deal. Either you talk to me now and let me try to help you, or you wait until he arrives and get yourself in a whole lot more trouble. Now, which is it to be?'

Kier thought about this and decided he had met enough policemen for one day.

'I'll talk to you,' he said. 'But can I tell you a secret first?'

Doyle frowned.

'What do you mean?'

Kier leaned forward, beckoning to him across the table.

'I need to whisper it.'

Still frowning, Doyle sat down and leaned across the table.

'Sorry,' Kier whispered, 'it's nothing personal.'

Then, tucking his thumb carefully beneath Doyle's neck, he tapped him on the temple just the way Chiang had shown him. As the man's eyes flickered shut, Kier lowered Doyle's head gently down on to the desk.

'Sweet dreams,' he said.

But he knew Doyle wouldn't be out for long.

Two minutes was all he had.

FIFTEEN

Closing the door behind him, Kier walked quickly past a room where shirt-sleeved officers were busy tapping away at their keyboards or talking on the phone. When he reached the security door, he punched in the number he had memorised and heard the click of the catch opening.

As he walked into the reception area, the desk sergeant looked up. For a brief moment, they stared at each other. Then the sergeant dropped his pen, leapt to his feet and Kier ran for the door. Outside there were four steps down to the car park, but Kier didn't touch any of them. He hit the ground at the bottom and kept on running. He saw two uniformed officers walking towards him and for a moment he was tempted to head for the street. But he knew he wouldn't get far without a fight and he figured there'd been enough of that for one day. Besides, Frankie had taught him that the more distance you can get at the start, the better your chance of escape. Feeling for the keys in his pocket, he guessed the driver hadn't realised they were gone yet.

Oh well, he thought. *He soon will.*

Sprinting across the car park, he pushed the button on the key fob and heard the locks thump open.

'Hey!' yelled the sergeant from the top of the steps. 'Stop him!'

The two other officers looked up from their conversation and then broke into a run. Diving across the bonnet of the car, Kier rolled over and pulled open the door on the driver's side. Throwing himself in, he flicked the door catch and the locks thumped shut just as the sergeant reached the car. Ignoring the shouts and bangs on the door, Kier fired up the motor and slammed the gearstick into reverse. Pulling the steering wheel hard around to the right, he glanced in his rear-view mirror and saw the two other officers dive clear as he screeched out of the parking space. Stamping on the brake, he shifted into first and was about to release the clutch when the sergeant stepped up to the car and swung his baton.

The windshield shattered, crystallising into a curtain of broken glass. Punching a hole through it with his fist, Kier saw he had a clear run to the gate.

As the sergeant swung his baton again, spraying the side window all over the passenger seat, Kier let the clutch out and the car leapt forward in a squeal of smoking rubber. Swinging out into the road, he dabbed briefly at the brakes and then floored the accelerator. As he approached the end of the road, the cars in front of him slowed to a stop as the traffic lights turned red.

Damn it.

Blocked by the cars in front, Kier applied the brakes and glanced in the rear-view mirror to see several police officers running down the road towards him. A patrol car nosed its way out into the road with blue lights flashing and, for the first time since his arrest, Kier was worried. Until now he'd always had the advantage of surprise. But now they knew what they were dealing with, they weren't going to mess around.

Scanning the dashboard, Kier flicked a switch and was rewarded with the whoop-whoop of the siren, sound waves bouncing off walls and windows. As the cars in front pulled over he edged into the bus lane, slipped through a gap in the line of slow-moving traffic and accelerated past, siren wailing and blue lights flashing. He saw the other patrol car pull out behind him and knew his chances of escape were fading fast. An alert would already have gone out over the radio; police vehicles all over London would be performing U-turns, while helicopters checked their co-ordinates, all searching for a juvenile bank robber who thought he could steal a police car and get away with it.

What a mess, thought Kier. Jackson was not going to be pleased.

People were staring now, shoppers gazing open-mouthed as Kier headed up Brompton Road with the wind in his face, peering through the smashed windscreen in search of possibilities.

There was a small park over to his right and for a moment he considered bailing out, but there were few trees and even fewer people. The road swung around to the right and as he hit the bend he increased his speed slightly, hoping to put some distance between himself and the car behind. Up ahead he could see the green and gold canopies of Harrods department store, and beyond it a police van stopping the traffic.

It was now or never.

Stamping on the brakes, Kier flung the door open and ran. The pavement was crowded with shoppers and, after knocking into a newspaper seller, he veered right down Hans Road, suddenly finding himself outside the entrance of Harrods. Glancing over his shoulder, he saw police officers running around the corner and quickly slipped past the doorman into the food hall.

It was mid-afternoon and the place was quiet, with just a few shoppers milling about beneath the chandeliers, gazing at neat piles of beautiful food that most of them probably couldn't afford. Kier ran past the displays of exotic sweets and coloured candy sticks, skidding around a golden mountain of chocolate coins before reaching the escalator and leaping up the moving staircase three steps at a time.

He found himself in a room full of expensive-looking luggage; to one side he saw tiny puffed-up handbags dripping with gold perched on columns like sacred objects. A few well-dressed ladies were moving slowly between them, pausing among the shrines to admire and worship. But Kier wasn't interested in handbags. He was interested in the fact that the young woman at the glass service counter was walking away from it. He watched her make her way towards a customer on the far side of the room and waited until she had engaged her in conversation. Then he walked quickly across to where she had been standing, picked up the phone and dropped down behind the counter at the same moment that two policemen appeared at the top of the escalator.

Huddled next to a box marked *Gucci*, Kier punched in 9 for an outside line and then phoned Saskia's number.

'Come on,' he whispered as he heard a woman's voice say: 'He was here just a few seconds ago.'

The sound of footsteps disappeared rapidly across the shop floor and then Saskia was on the line asking, 'Yes? Who is this?'

'It's me. Kier.'

'Kier? Where are you?'

'I'm in Harrods.'

'*Harrods?*'

'Listen. I'm in trouble. I need help.'

'OK.' Saskia's voice was calm and focused, but there was an edge to it. 'What kind of help?'

'The kind that will get me out of here without half the Metropolitan Police force noticing.'

There was a pause on the other end of the line.

'Saskia?'

'OK. What floor are you on now?'

'First.'

'Right. Make your way to the ladies' toilets and I'll be there as soon as I can.'

'What? Saskia, I—'

But the line had gone dead and Kier could hear the sound of high heels tapping their way across the floor towards him. He replaced the phone and looked up to see the shop assistant staring at him with one eyebrow raised.

'Can I help you?' she asked.

'I very much doubt it,' said Kier.

Then he dropped the phone and ran.

SIXTEEN

He made it as far as the audio-visual department before they caught up with him. As two police officers walked towards him past walls of flat-screen TVs, a voice behind him said, 'All right, son. Stay where you are.'

Kier looked over his shoulder and saw that another two policemen were approaching from behind. Rubbing the floor with the sole of his foot, he came to a decision. Not perfect of course, but it would have to do.

The men in front of him were moving cautiously, anxious not to startle him into a run, and he knew that the men behind him would be doing the same. He guessed they'd be feeling pretty confident right now. After all, there were four of them and one of him. How hard could it be?

Kier pressed the toes of his right foot against the heel of his trainer and slipped it off. Then he did the same with the other one, bending over and hooking his fingers into the heels. He peered through his knees at the two men approaching him from behind, then stood up again.

'Are you Richard Smith?' asked the officer in front of him as he was joined by his colleague.

Kier held the shoes up on either side of his head and waggled them back and forth.

'No,' he said. 'I'm Mickey Mouse.'

He waited until they were just over an arm's length away. Then, whipping his arms down hard and fast, he released his grip and the shoes flew backwards like stones from a slingshot. Hearing the startled cries from behind him as the shoes met their targets, he saw the surprise on the faces of the two men in front of him and smiled.

'Squeak, squeak,' he said.

Then he leapt forward, put his hands on their shoulders and swung himself between them. As his socks slid him smoothly across the polished floor, he tensed his stomach muscles, shifted his weight forward and, before the laws of physics had time to slow him down, he was up and running through the door.

'Excuse me,' he said to the startled woman as he skidded into the ladies' toilets. 'I think I must have got the wrong room.'

Noticing that the doors to the individual cubicles were open and that there was no one else in the room, he followed her out and waited until she had disappeared around the corner. Then he re-entered the toilets and caught sight of himself in the mirror.

'Don't look at me like that,' he said. 'It was Saskia's idea.'

Making his way into one of the cubicles, he bolted the door and sat down to wait.

After a while he heard the door squeak open, followed by the sound of two women talking.

'What is it, do you think?'

'Maybe a bomb scare or something.'

'No, I don't think so. If it was a bomb scare, they'd have evacuated the whole store by now.'

'I don't know then. But it must be pretty serious. The place is absolutely crawling with police.'

Kier listened as they reapplied their make-up and the more he heard, the more he realised Saskia needed to get here quickly. There was obviously no shortage of police officers doing their shopping in Harrods and they would almost certainly be watching the entrances and searching the building, floor by floor. Once they discovered he wasn't out there, it wouldn't take a genius to think of sending someone up for a quick cubicle check.

In which case, how was Saskia being here going to help?

Deciding he needed an alternative plan, Kier stood on the toilet seat and examined the window. It was made of a single pane of frosted glass; not too thick and, if it came to it, easy enough to break.

Hooking his arm through the small window at the top, he swivelled his wrist and raised his arm at an angle of forty-five degrees to the glass.

'Kier,' said a voice, 'if you're about to do what I think you're about to do, then . . . don't.'

Kier spun around to see Saskia resting her chin on the top of the adjacent cubicle. Her neat, shoulder-length hair was dark and shiny as blackberries and her eyes were the kind of butterscotch brown that reminded people of kittens or puppy dogs. But Kier wasn't fooled for a minute. He could tell right away that she wasn't in a puppy-dog kind of mood.

'Saskia,' he said, pulling his hand back through the window. 'I didn't hear you come in.'

'Of course you didn't,' said Saskia, her eyes glittering angrily. 'Because you're an idiot, that's why. With less sense than you were born with.'

'Nice to see you too,' said Kier. 'What took you so long?'

Saskia narrowed her eyes. 'I was twenty-eight minutes. Which, when you consider I had to stop off and buy a few things first, was pretty damn good, don't you think?'

'What kind of things?'

'Things for you.'

Saskia swung herself over the top of the cubicle, landed neatly in front of Kier and handed him a large green Harrods bag. She was wearing a dark blue, box-pleated skirt, white knee-length socks and a blue and white gingham blouse. On her feet she wore a pair of flat, sensible court shoes. She looked exactly like a schoolgirl on her lunch break.

Kier grinned.

'You look nice,' he said.

'Yeah, that's it,' said Saskia, 'go ahead and laugh. Then take a look in the bag.'

Kier picked up the Harrods bag and peered inside. He pulled out a dark blue, box-pleated skirt, a pair of white knee-length socks and a short-sleeved summer blouse complete with light blue stripes. At the bottom was a box containing a pair of flat, sensible court shoes. Beneath that was a blonde wig.

'Oh, no way,' said Kier, shaking his head. 'You have got to be kidding.'

Saskia unbolted the door and walked towards the washbasins. Then she turned back, smiled and held up a small container of eyeshadow.

'Whenever you're ready, sweetie,' she said.

SEVENTEEN

Kier stared at himself in the mirror. He shut his eyes and opened them again. But she was still there, the blonde schoolgirl with the blue eyeshadow, staring right back at him.

Saskia grinned.

'Look who's here,' she said. 'It's the lovely Kiera.'

Kier gave her a sarcastic smile.

'Ha ha. Very funny.'

The door swung open and a woman police officer walked in.

'Hello, girls,' she said, turning to look at the row of cubicles. 'Have you been in here long?'

'Not long. About five minutes, I guess.'

The policewoman peered into the cubicles.

'Any idea who this bag belongs to?'

The bag. Damn.

'It's mine,' said Kier, doing his best to sound soft and husky.

Saskia gave him a look which suggested he wasn't really pulling it off, so he walked quickly back to the cubicle and squeezed past the WPC.

'Thanks, officer,' he said, retrieving the bag with what he hoped was a suitably girlish giggle.

Saskia raised her eyes skywards, but Kier was relieved to see that the shoebox was the last thing he had put back in the bag, hiding the clothes underneath.

'Have you seen anything strange at all, since you've been here?' asked the WPC.

A hijacked crashed police car, thought Kier. *Four police officers lying on the floor of the audio-visual department. Myself dressed as a schoolgirl.*

'Not really, no.'

'Nothing at all?'

'Come to think of it,' said Saskia, 'I did see a boy running through the toy department. He seemed to be in quite a hurry.'

The WPC perked up at this.

'When?'

'Oh, I don't know. A few minutes ago. Just before we came in.'

Saskia followed this up with an innocent, *Why, do you think that might be useful?* kind of look, but the woman was already gabbling into her radio and heading out of the door.

'Don't mention it,' said Saskia as the door swung shut. 'I'm just happy to help.'

She looked at her watch and turned to Kier.

'What's going on, Kier?'

'I sort of got arrested.'

'Yeah, well, I guessed that much. What happened?'

'I, erm . . . got involved in the bank robbery.'

'You went *in* there?'

'I couldn't help it. There was this waitress and she—'

'Oh, I get it.' Saskia narrowed her eyes. 'Pretty, was she?'

'No. Yes. Kind of . . . Look, it doesn't matter. I just thought I could get her out, that's all. But then it got complicated. They had guns, Saskia. Someone could have been killed.'

'Including you.'

Kier gave her a smug look.

'No chance. Those guys were amateurs.'

'No, Kier.' Saskia grabbed his shoulder and spun him around angrily. '*You're* the amateur. Your problem is that you're fresh out of training and suddenly you think you know it all and no one can tell you anything. But see what happens when you don't listen?'

'Yeah,' said Kier. 'I stop a bank robbery.'

'Oh, right. Well done.' Saskia folded her arms. 'You stopped a bank robbery which probably would have been stopped anyway and now you've got half the Metropolitan Police force out looking for you. That's brilliant, Kier. Give out the pencils.'

Kier caught sight of himself in the mirror and saw that, beneath the blonde wig, he was wearing a rather shamefaced expression. It was irritating. Saskia suddenly seemed to have developed a knack of making him feel like a five-year-old.

'Did you manage to take some pictures?'

'Yeah, but I shot the phone up.'

'Great.'

'OK, I admit it. I messed up. But there was no sign of the guy in the photograph. And there was something else I noticed.'

'Go on.'

'The police were there very quickly.'

'Wow. Amazing. Well, at least someone's doing their job properly.'

'No, I mean incredibly quickly. Like one minute after the cashier pressed the alarm.'

'So?'

'So they turned up fully armed and ready for action, Saskia. It wasn't a surprise to them. No way. They *knew* this robbery was going down.'

'Hmmm.' Saskia nodded thoughtfully. 'Maybe that is interesting. Have you told Jackson yet?'

Kier gave her a look. 'I've been a bit busy, to be honest.'

Kier counted at least eleven police officers as they made their way back through the store.

'Saskia,' he whispered when they reached the toy department. 'Those guys by the giant panda. They saw me before. They know what I look like.'

The men – who had been on the receiving end of Kier's shoe trick – were moving carefully through the store, checking every customer. Kier noticed one of them had a swelling under his left eye.

'Saskia?'

'Relax, Kier. Just keep talking to me, OK? Remember, you're a schoolgirl. And schoolgirls are not what those guys are looking for.'

'OK,' said Kier under his breath. 'I'm a schoolgirl, I'm a schoolgirl . . .'

'So tell me,' said Saskia, 'what do you think of Gabriella's new hair extensions? I mean, hello? What is *up* with that?'

Kier pointed to his wig. 'Don't talk hair,' he said.

'Oh, OK. Are you going to Jennifer's party tonight?'

'Oh, shut *up*!' said Kier, trying to make his voice

high and soft. 'Of *course* I'm going. I wouldn't miss it. All those *hot* guys and stuff!'

'OK,' said Saskia. 'Don't overdo it.'

'Hello, ladies,' said the officer with the swollen eye. 'We're looking for a boy of about thirteen, maybe fourteen.'

'Aren't we all?' said Kier, fluttering his eyelashes. 'Join the club.'

'Take no notice of her, Officer,' said Saskia hurriedly. 'I think the heat must be getting to her.'

'Yeah, well,' said the man, tugging at his shirt collar. 'I know how she feels.'

He looked at Kier and studied his face for a moment or two.

'You look kind of familiar,' he said. 'Don't I know you from somewhere?'

Kier mentally measured out the distance. He could sweep the guy's legs out from underneath him no problem; they'd be gone before the man even hit the floor. But Saskia was glaring at him, sending out signals, and he decided against it.

'Oh, I don't think so. I must just have one of those faces.'

The man kept staring, so Kier turned to Saskia and said, 'Marie, what time did you say you have to be at the dentist?'

Saskia's hand flew up to her mouth and she said,

'Oh, my gosh, it's a quarter past two and I'm supposed to be there at half past! Will you excuse us, Officer?'

The officer smiled and said, 'Sure, no problem,' because the girl was pretty and nice and of course she needed to get to the dentist on time. In fact, he was still smiling seven seconds later when it suddenly occurred to him why her friend looked so familiar.

'Wait!' he shouted, spinning round on his heel.

But there was no sign of them. The two girls had completely disappeared and, in spite of the tight security cordon around the store, not a single person could recall seeing them go.

EIGHTEEN

Locking himself into a toilet cubicle in Euston station, Kier quickly changed into the clothes Saskia had picked out for him in a charity shop: a pair of jeans two sizes too big, a plastic belt to hold them up, a T-shirt with the words *Allied Carpets* written on the front, a baggy jumper with patches on the elbows and a pair of cheap trainers with torn insoles and frayed laces.

'Get yourself a clean phone,' she'd told him, 'and call Jackson when you've changed.' Then she was gone again, melting away into the crowd before he'd had a chance to reply.

He unwrapped the cheap Pay As You Go phone and stuffed the packaging into a carrier bag, along with the wig and school uniform. Anyone trying to trace his calls now would only find the name of Jack Smith on the paperwork. Not very original perhaps, but it would have to do.

Unlocking the door again, he went across to the

basins and ran the taps, cupping his hands beneath them and dumping water on his head. He messed his hair up with his fingers, then knelt beneath the hand-drier, teasing the strands of hair between his fingers until they stuck out in all directions.

'Oh yeah,' he said to his scarecrow reflection. 'You've got it going *on*.'

But it was obvious that the ladies in the charity shop took their work seriously; the clothes, although cheap and old, had still been washed and ironed. According to Saskia, the next part of his mission required him to look as if he'd been living rough on the streets for a while. If he wanted to appear convincing, there was still some work to be done.

After scouring the backstreets for ten minutes, he came across a builder's skip and quickly threw in the bag containing the clothes and phone packaging. Checking that no one was watching, he climbed in and stretched out across the piles of chipped plaster-board and broken bricks, rolling around until his clothes were covered in a fine layer of dust. Hooking the arm of his sweater on to a nail, he ripped the sleeve in two places. Then he rubbed his hands on an old bike chain and wiped his fingers across his jeans.

'Hey!' said a voice. 'What the hell are you doing?'

Kier looked up to see a builder peering over the side of the skip.

'I'm taking a dust bath,' he said. 'You know. Like the birds.'

The builder stared at him.

'Are you a nutter or something?'

Kier nodded. 'Yeah. I think I probably am.'

'Well, go and be a nutter somewhere else,' said the builder, throwing a plank of wood into the end of the skip. 'Some of us have got work to do.'

'You and me both,' said Kier.

He climbed out and stared at himself in a window. He now looked like someone who had slept in a skip. Like someone who'd been rolling around in one, in fact.

'I know I'm an idiot,' said Kier, when Jackson answered the phone. 'You don't have to tell me.'

'I don't think you're an idiot,' said Jackson. 'Impetuous, yes. But that's a very different thing.'

In the background Kier could hear the chirruping of cicadas and imagined Jackson sitting beneath his sunshade, cup of tea in hand.

'So, I gather the police were rather quick to arrive?'

'Yeah, less than five minutes.' Kier had detected a note of concern in Jackson's voice. 'Why, do you think they've got something to do with it?'

'It's probably nothing. But I think it's best not to

involve them any more than we have to at this stage, hmm?'

'OK.' Kier reddened, knowing this was Jackson's way of telling him not to mess up again. 'Sorry about that.'

'All right. I want you to head south of the river and check out an area near Putney Bridge. It's a stretch of about a kilometre, just west of Wandsworth Park. But listen, it's the same place your dad was working just before he was killed, so you need to be careful. Keep your head down and stay low-profile, OK?'

Kier glanced at his ripped sweater and oil-stained jeans.

'I don't think that'll be a problem,' he said.

'When you get there, look out for any drug deals going down. If you can, buy some coke and test it with the swabs we gave you. If it's genuine, find out where they live and then we can tag them 24/7, find out who's supplying them and hopefully who the guy in the photo is.'

'Is that it?' asked Kier, who had been hoping for something a bit more interesting. 'Is that all you want me to do?'

'Patience is a virtue,' said Jackson. 'Didn't Chiang teach you that?'

* * *

It was dark when Kier joined the queue outside the soup kitchen. He'd been walking up and down for several hours and the nearest he'd come to a crime was some old guy spitting on the pavement. It was hardly Crime Central.

'Ain't seen you round here before,' said a voice.

Kier turned to see a man in a shabby coat and wellington boots standing behind him. He had the squashed nose and cauliflower ears of a man who has been in plenty of fights and lost most of them.

'I'm new,' said Kier.

The man nodded.

'We were all new once. But you'd best not let on. There are people here who'll take advantage.'

'What kind of people?'

The man shrugged.

'All kinds. Just watch your back.'

'Thanks. I'll do that.'

As the queue shuffled forward, Kier noticed two men step out from the shadows beneath the bridge. As he watched, a third man stopped and thrust his hand forward as if he was handing something over. It looked promising but Kier didn't want to appear too interested, so he turned his attention back to the lights of the van.

'What's your name son?' asked the guy with the squashed nose.

'Jack,' said Kier, remembering the form in the phone shop.

'What's yours?'

'Nuggy.'

'Well, Nuggy . . .' Kier held out his hand. 'It's good to meet you, I guess.'

Nuggy gripped his hand and Kier felt the firm, angry remains of years spent going nowhere.

'Take my advice, Jack. Stay away from those people.'

'What people?'

'I saw the way you were looking at 'em. They'll make you believe heaven's waiting right around the corner, but take my word for it, kid – hell's the only place they're heading. And they'll take you with 'em, easy as blinking.'

'How do you know?' asked Kier.

'Because,' said Nuggy, 'I've been there.'

And it was only then, as he looked into Nuggy's eyes, that Kier caught a brief glimpse of the man he might have been, a man who didn't want Kier to tread the path he had taken.

When they reached the van, Nuggy pushed Kier in front of him and pointed at a cup of soup on the counter.

'There you go, kid. Put some meat on your bones.'

'Thanks.' Kier passed a cup back to Nuggy and then took one for himself.

'You know what I dreamed last night?' asked Nuggy. 'I dreamed I turned up here and they were serving pizza. With extra anchovies.'

'Dream on,' said the thin, bearded man behind the counter. He turned to Kier. 'This your first night?'

'First of many, I guess,' said Kier.

He took a sip from the cup and tasted watery vegetable soup.

'Where are you staying?'

Kier shrugged. 'I haven't figured that one out yet.'

'Under the bridge is best,' said a pale man with dirt under his nails. 'Reckon we can make room for a littl'un.'

'What about them?' asked Kier, nodding towards the figures beneath the bridge.

'They won't stay long,' said Nuggy. 'They'll do their business and then they'll be gone.'

'Business?' asked Kier. 'What kind of business?'

The pale man chuckled. 'Bit wet behind the ears this one, ain't he? They're dealers, kid. If your money's good, they'll get you anything you want. So it's kind of lucky you ain't got no money. Cos that's all those scumbags are interested in. If you ain't got money, they'll leave you alone.'

Kier thought of the roll of banknotes concealed in his sock and decided to play this one carefully.

'Hang on,' he said. 'I just need the toilet. I'll be back in a minute.'

Walking up the steps to the main street, he took two twenties from his sock and folded them into his sleeve before cutting along the top of the embankment and past the bridge. When he reached the far side, he climbed down again and approached the bridge from the opposite direction. The two men were already talking to someone else and Kier waited while they exchanged something with him. As he disappeared into the night, Kier walked beneath the bridge and stopped in the shadows. He saw that both men were wearing sweatshirts with the hoods pulled over their heads.

'Hi,' he said. 'Nice evening.'

'Just keep walking, street boy,' said the larger man, 'if you know what's good for you.'

'I *do* know what's good for me as a matter of fact,' said Kier, moving closer. 'How about you sell me some?'

The second man curled his lip into a vicious sneer.

'You think you can afford what we're selling?'

'Maybe,' said Kier. 'Maybe I got lucky.'

As he watched them move closer, Kier measured

the distance between them in his mind. They were hard men, no doubt about it, although their heavy bulk meant it would be easy enough to catch them off balance if required. But, the last thing he wanted to do was blow his cover. He would definitely have to play this one carefully.

The first man grabbed Kier's jumper and shoved him back against the brickwork.

'Are you wasting my time?' he hissed, his face so close that Kier could smell the stale smoke and alcohol. 'Is that what you're doing?'

'No,' said Kier, resisting the urge to break the man's grip and show him how these things should really be done.

'Well, that's what it feels like,' said the man, pulling his fist back. 'And we hate people wasting our time, don't we, Ryan?'

Whoever Ryan was, he nodded and grinned.

'We sure do, Maggot.'

Ryan and Maggot, thought Kier. *Sounds like some third-rate cop show.*

'I've got money,' said Kier, pulling the two twenties from his sleeve. 'I just wanted to buy some stuff, that's all.'

'Oh yeah?' Maggot's eyes flashed nastily as he snatched the money from Kier's hand. 'What kind of stuff?'

'What have you got?'

Maggot grinned so that Kier could see the gaps between his teeth.

'Nothing for you,' he said, tucking the money into the pocket of his jeans. 'In fact the only thing you're buying is the chance to walk away from here without a broken nose.'

'All right,' said Kier, trying one last shot, 'but you gotta help me. I don't want to live like this no more. I see you guys in your smart clothes and trainers and I want to be a dealer like you. Please. Just tell me how to get started.'

Kier was so caught up with the acting that when Maggot's fist slammed into his stomach he was completely unprepared and doubled over as if he'd been shot. Then Ryan stepped forward and Kier went down in a flurry of punches, curling himself up into a ball while he thought about what he should do next. Although he didn't want to blow his cover, he really didn't want his head used for football practice either.

He decided to cut his losses and go for their knees when suddenly the kicking stopped and Maggot pulled him to his feet again.

'Now get this straight,' he said. 'This is our patch and no one moves in on it. *No one*. Understand?'

'Yeah,' said Kier, wiping blood from his mouth. 'I got that.'

As the punches began again, he decided enough was enough. He was just getting ready to knock the pair of them into the river when he heard the sound of voices and looked up to see Nuggy and a few of the other guys heading towards them.

'You boys want trouble?' Nuggy was shouting. 'I'll give you trouble.'

He began rolling up his sleeves and Kier could see the faded blue tattoos swirling across his forearms.

The two men stopped what they were doing and turned to face Nuggy.

'Stay away, old man,' said Maggot. 'This ain't none of your business.'

'Well, maybe I want to make it my business,' said Nuggy, still walking.

'Your choice,' said Maggot.

He reached into his pocket, pulled out a gun and pointed it straight at Nuggy's head. As Nuggy stopped, Maggot smiled a thin nasty smile.

'What's the matter, old man? Changed your mind?'

'Leave the kid alone,' said Nuggy. 'Just let him go.'

'Here's an idea. Why don't you come over here and make me?'

Kier saw the madness glittering in Maggot's eyes and knew he wasn't bluffing. But Nuggy continued to stand his ground.

'You want to shoot me? Then go right ahead. But remember, the police don't bother too much with us down here at the moment.'

'What's that s'posed to mean?'

'It means that if they find an old man with a bullet in his head, it's gonna make them look bad. So then they'll come around kicking a few dustbins until they find someone to blame. And while that's happening, all your customers are going to vanish into thin air.'

'He could be right,' said Ryan.

'Shut up,' said Maggot. 'Just shut up.'

'Leave it,' said Ryan. 'It's not worth it.'

Maggot thought for a moment. Then he turned and pointed the gun at Kier.

'You,' he said. 'Get up.'

Kier saw Maggot's finger twitch on the trigger and wasn't about to argue.

'Don't do anything stupid,' Kier said, putting his hands in the air.

'Like what?' asked Maggot. 'Like letting you live, you mean?'

'No, you can do that,' said Kier. 'That'd be absolutely fine.'

'Yeah, you just keep going with that mouth of yours,' said Maggot. 'Keep going and make me do it.'

Looking at the twisted smile on his face, Kier couldn't decide whether Maggot was going to pull the trigger or not. But one thing he did he know: for all the incredible things Chiang had taught him, none of them would be any use once the bullet left the gun. The only thing that mattered was speed, so—

'Hey!' shouted Maggot.

But as he pulled the trigger, there was only empty space where Kier had been standing, and while Maggot shouted and cursed, Kier was zigzagging his way up the path, already trying to figure out what his next move was going to be.

NINETEEN

It was just after midnight when Kier checked into a cheap hotel near Paddington station. The man on reception eyed him suspiciously, but when Kier put three twenty-pound notes on the counter he handed over the room key and went back to reading his paper.

Kier took a shower and called Jackson.

'Did you get anything?' Jackson asked.

'Yeah, a good kicking,' said Kier. 'But don't worry, I can sort it. I just need to do things differently next time.'

There was a pause on the other end of the line.

'Kier, it sounds as if you've been compromised. If you go back now they'll be suspicious. I think we should let Saskia handle this.'

'What?'

Kier walked to the window and stared at the ribbon of tail lights outside, annoyed by the implication that he wasn't up to the job.

'Look, it was dark and I was dressed like someone who lives in a skip. They won't recognise me next time, I can guarantee it.'

'There are no guarantees in this game, Kier. Just tell me where you are and I'll send Saskia along. I'm not saying you can't do it, but you've become too involved. I just think you need to back off for a while.'

'No,' said Kier quietly, 'I'm not backing off. These people killed my father and I'm going to make them pay for it.'

'Kier, you can't let—'

'Tell Saskia to meet me tomorrow night at the Hilton Hotel on Park Lane. Let's say eleven o'clock in the foyer. And tell her she needs to look *expensive*.'

'Kier, listen. You're not—'

'Sorry, you're breaking up. I'll call you tomorrow.'

'Kier—'

Kier ended the call and switched off his phone.

He turned on the TV and spent the next five minutes switching channels, trying to take the edge off his anger. Eventually he fell asleep watching some programme about dwarf lantern sharks. He woke up to hear someone explaining that they were no bigger than a packet of biscuits.

'I did not know that,' he said.

Then he turned off the TV and went to sleep.

★ ★ ★

The next morning he went shopping and purchased a pair of khaki chinos, a brown snakeskin belt, a pale blue shirt with button-down collar, a dark navy blazer with yellow pinstripes and some expensive leather shoes.

The plan was ambitious, no doubt about it. And if it worked, then the big boys would show up tonight – maybe even the guy from the photograph. And then Kier could tail them back to wherever they came from and finally prove to Jackson that he was just as good as Saskia, although he still hoped she'd come along as backup. But in case she didn't, and in case things didn't work out quite as planned, he bought a length of washing line and some secateurs from a high-street store. Not exactly top-quality handcuffs, but they'd do the job if things got rough.

Then, because the sun was shining and he had nothing to do until evening, he took a detour through Hyde Park, watching parents buying ice creams for their children and spreading picnic rugs out beneath the trees.

He thought of his father then, and of Jackson's lost son.

And as he watched the children playing in the sunshine he knew that, if he could pull this off, it might just keep the shadows away from them for a little while longer.

* * *

As the day cooled into evening, he stopped off at the Pizza Express on Beauchamp Place and ordered a Sloppy Giuseppe with extra cheese. He sat at a table for one, drinking a double shot from the espresso bar and checking his messages. There were three of them, all from Jackson, all telling him to call back. But there was no mention of Saskia, so he turned his phone off again and watched the world go by, waiting for the sun to go down.

At around nine-fifteen he booked himself a bedroom suite at the Hilton on the twenty-sixth floor. It was jaw-droppingly expensive, but he needed to make a good impression. Besides, Jackson was paying and he could definitely afford it.

The bedroom suite looked suitably expensive too, but rather naff, as if it had been decorated by someone from *Antiques Roadshow*. There were several gold-framed paintings on the wall, a big double bed with tasselled cushions and a television concealed in a dark hardwood cabinet. Next to the TV was a dressing table with ornate gold handles and on top was a fruit bowl piled high with shiny red apples. But every inch of the place – from the marble bathroom to the Regency-striped armchair – shouted *money*, which was exactly the effect Kier was after.

After stashing the secateurs and washing line under the bed, Kier took the elevator back to the lobby and checked his reflection in the mirror. A bit of pizza topping had somehow found its way on to the arm of his blazer, but otherwise he looked exactly as he wanted to look: a well-dressed teenager who could afford the good things in life.

People were already queuing outside the soup kitchen when Kier arrived. He didn't think he would be recognised, but it wasn't worth the risk. Skirting around through the backstreets, he approached the bridge from the far side.

The men were skulking in the shadows as before, two trapdoor spiders waiting to pounce. Kier decided that confidence was the key. After all, it was dark and he was dressed completely differently; he just needed to play the part.

'Hi,' he said. 'I'm looking for some of the good stuff.'

Maggot stepped out of the shadows and stared at him. For a moment, Kier wondered if his new clothes would do their job, but then Maggot said suspiciously, 'What kind of stuff?' and Kier knew he was in business.

'You know.' Kier thought back to the drug identification session he'd had in Crete before leaving. 'Party stuff. Nose candy. Co*caine*.'

He noticed Maggot kept one hand tucked inside his pocket and knew what that was about. He would definitely deal with that one first if it came to it.

Maggot looked him up and down, thinking about the money he was going to make.

'I can do you a couple of grams. But it's gonna cost you.'

'How much?'

'Sixty pounds a gram.'

Kier knew the going rate was more like forty and didn't want to appear naïve.

'That's a bit steep, isn't it?'

'Take it or leave it.'

'What if I wanted more than a couple of grams? Would that bring the price down?'

Kier knew he was playing a risky game. But if he was going to get to the big boys, the stakes needed to be higher.

'How much more?'

Kier swallowed and concentrated on keeping his heart rate level.

'About a kilo?'

'A *kilo*?' Maggot curled his lip. 'Get out of here.'

'I'm serious.'

He watched Ryan step out of the shadows and guessed that, if there was money to be made, Ryan didn't want to miss out.

'Oh, you're serious?' Ryan was determined to join in now. 'And where's a kid like you gonna get that kind of money?'

'From my trust fund.'

'Your *trust* fund?'

'Yeah. My dad likes me to have the good things in life. It's my girlfriend's sixteenth birthday tomorrow night and she's having a party. So I thought I'd make sure there was enough of the good stuff to go round, if you know what I mean. A kilo should do it, don't you think?'

Maggot narrowed his eyes.

'You know you're talking serious money here?'

'Yeah. But not as serious as sixty quid a gram. If I'm buying in bulk, then I'm looking for a discount.'

'Is that right?' Maggot licked his lips until they glistened with spit. 'What kind of discount?'

'I'll give you thirty grand for the lot.'

Kier could see the excitement in Maggot's eyes at the thought of all that money. But he was greedy for more.

'That's a fifty per cent discount.'

'Only at your prices. And I'm talking cash up front. No messing.'

Maggot looked at Ryan and when Ryan nodded Kier knew he had them hooked. But reeling them in wasn't going to be easy.

'It ain't a problem for us,' said Maggot, 'but it might be a problem for you. How are you going to get your hands on that kind of money?'

'Maybe you should let me worry about that,' said Kier.

'Maybe you should watch what you're getting into,' said Maggot. 'This ain't no high school musical. If you want this stuff, we're going to need to talk to some pretty important people. The kind of people who get upset when they don't get paid on time, if you know what I mean.'

'The money will be there,' said Kier. 'But I'm going to need the stuff tonight.'

'Tonight?'

'Uh-huh.'

'Can't we just bring it along to your girlfriend's party?'

'Oh yeah, good idea.' Kier raised an eyebrow. 'You think her dad's just going to let a couple of dealers walk in and start handing out charlie?'

'OK. Give us a couple of hours and we'll have the stuff here.'

'Not here,' said Kier. 'Bring it to my hotel room.'

'Why not here?'

'Well, I don't know about you,' said Kier, 'but it's not the kind of place I'd want to go walking around with thirty grand in my pocket. I mean,' he added, looking at Ryan, 'you never know who you're going to meet.'

'OK. So where's your hotel?'

'The Hilton on Park Lane.'

'Very nice.'

'Yeah, it is. The room number is four hundred and thirty-six. I'll have the money there in a couple of hours. But if you're not there by midnight, I'll go shopping elsewhere.' He looked at Maggot and smiled. 'If you know what I mean.'

He could tell that Maggot really, really wanted to hit him. But he wanted the money even more. So he just nodded and said, 'We'll be there, don't worry.'

'Good,' said Kier, turning back the way he had come. 'In that case I'll see you later.'

'Wait,' said Maggot, peering at Kier from the depths of his hood. 'Don't I know you from some-where?'

'No,' said Kier, remembering the conversation he'd had with the policeman in Harrods. 'I think I just have one of those faces.'

Then, before Maggot and his brain could start working things out, Kier walked up the path and disappeared into the night.

TWENTY

At around ten minutes to eleven, Kier folded his arms and looked at the bundles of notes he had piled up on the dressing table. Although there were nine thousand pounds here – more or less all that was left of the ten thousand he had arrived with – it didn't look nearly as impressive as he'd hoped. In fact, any self-respecting drug dealer would figure out pretty quickly that it was about twenty thousand short.

Kier stepped back and tapped his teeth with his fingernail.

It would have to do.

In the lobby he checked the clock and saw that it was gone eleven.

'Are you waiting for someone?' asked the concierge.

'Yeah, I'm waiting for a girl. She's dark-haired,

about sixteen, big brown eyes and, erm, hopefully dressed to kill. You haven't seen her by any chance, have you?'

The concierge shook his head. 'I'm sure I would remember a girl like that,' he said.

'I'm sure you would,' said Kier.

He gazed out of the entrance, but all he could see was a road full of late-night traffic.

'If you do see her, can you tell her I'm in room four hundred and thirty-six?'

'Four hundred and thirty-six. Of course, sir.'

Kier took a last look out at the street and then headed for the elevator. Maybe she hadn't got the message. Maybe Jackson had decided not to send her after all.

Either way, it looked as if Kier would be doing this alone.

Back in his hotel room, he put the money in the drawer of the dressing table. He tried the balcony doors, but they were locked and there was no key. Taking a paperclip from the hotel information folder, he undid the security lock and opened it, feeling cool air on his face and hearing the sounds of the street from below.

He turned on the news and saw that house prices were down, unemployment was up and a beluga whale called Nack had learned the Japanese word for 'bucket'.

He watched the forecast and saw that the good weather was set to continue.

Then he turned off the TV and waited.

At 11.28 there was a knock at the door.

Kier guessed three, maybe four of them. He really hoped one would be the guy from the photograph.

He took a slow, deep breath.

Then he opened the door.

Maggot was standing there with his arms folded and Ryan stood behind him with a small rucksack slung over his shoulder.

No one else was with them.

Maggot grinned.

'Did you think we weren't coming?'

'No,' said Kier. 'I knew you'd come.'

He stood back to let them pass before making a quick check of the corridor, but they had definitely come alone.

Kier knew at once that he had miscalculated. In his mind he had imagined the promise of serious money would draw out the big boys. That they would come along to his hotel room and he would show them the cash, make out he was going to get some more and then trail them back to wherever they kept the stuff. But in his haste to complete his mission, he had overlooked one simple fact: Ryan and Maggot were driven by greed. They thought they were in line for the biggest payday of their lives, and they weren't about to share it with anyone else. Kier would have to think again. And he would have to do it fast.

'So,' said Maggot as Kier walked back into the room. 'Have you got the money?'

'Yeah, I've got it.'

'OK.' Maggot sat on the bed and leaned back against the headboard. He put his hands behind his head as if he owned the place. 'So where is it?'

'Show me the stuff first.'

Maggot looked at Ryan and nodded. Ryan unfastened the drawstrings on the top of his rucksack and pulled out a plastic carrier bag. He reached into the carrier bag, took out a brown-paper package and placed it on the bed. Kier took a step forwards, but Maggot moved his leg in front of it.

'Not so fast,' he said. 'You've seen ours, now let's see yours.'

'All I've seen is a brown-paper package,' said Kier. 'For all I know there could be half a dozen sausages in there.'

'What's the matter?' sneered Ryan. 'Don't you trust us?'

'Oh sure,' said Kier. 'Why wouldn't I?'

He opened the drawer of the dressing table a little way and pulled out a bundle of money.

'There,' he said, tossing it on the bed. 'That's just for openers.'

Ryan leaned forward to pick it up, but Maggot swung his legs over the side of the bed and got there before him.

'Well, let's see, shall we?' He thumbed through the notes in a way that suggested he was used to counting money. 'Five hundred pounds. That ain't gonna get you very far, is it?'

'Like I said, that's just for openers.'

Ryan moved around the bed and Kier saw that his fists were bunched, ready for use.

'Got some more tucked away with your make-up, have you?'

Kier pushed the dressing-table drawer shut.

'If you're not going to play fair,' he said, 'then I'm not going to play at all.'

'You're the one who wanted to buy it, kid,' said Ryan. 'Now you're going to find out how much it really costs.' He moved a step closer. 'Come on. Give me the money.'

Kier thought of still, clear water; of bright petals dancing across a stone floor.

'Why don't you make me?' he asked.

Ryan had obviously been a boxer at one time, because he moved quickly for a big man. Kier watched him lean slightly as if he was preparing to throw a stone, then swing his right fist hard and fast at Kier's head. Experience had taught Ryan that a punch like that would knock most people out before they even hit the ground.

But Kier was not most people.

Which meant that all Ryan's experience was about as much use to him as a concrete lifeboat.

Kier moved smoothly beneath the punch and turned slightly so that Ryan's momentum would unbalance him, waiting until the weight of Ryan's chest made contact with his shoulder before twisting fast and somersaulting him into the wall. Ryan hit the floor with a thump that shook the room but he was quickly on his feet again. As he ran at Kier like an angry bull, Kier calmly cupped his hand and waited until Ryan was nearly upon him. Then he flicked his arm out like a striking cobra and, as his fingertips struck Ryan's temple, Ryan staggered backwards and sank to the ground.

'Well, I'll be damned,' whispered Maggot as Ryan deflated like a punctured beach ball.

Kier turned to see that Maggot was standing by the balcony doors with the gun in his hand.

'I knew you looked familiar,' he said.

'Yeah, well,' said Kier, playing for time, 'I like to dress down once in a while.'

'What?' said Maggot, seeming confused.

And it was then, with a sickening feeling in his stomach, that Kier realised the truth. Maggot hadn't – as he had first thought – recognised him from their previous encounter beneath the bridge. He had recognised him because he had been there on the night when everything changed, standing at the end of the hospital corridor with a hood over his head and a gun in his hand.

'It was you,' said Kier. 'You were the one who killed my father.'

TWENTY-ONE

Maggot shook his head. 'Not me, my friend. As I remember it, I was too busy trying to kill you.'

With a sick feeling in his stomach, Kier stared at the man who had tried to take his life away.

'But why?'

Maggot smiled.

'Because you were there.'

Kier could feel his anger growing, dark tendrils twisting through his blood. He leaned back, resting his hand on the dressing table.

'So if you didn't kill him, who did?'

'Does it matter?'

'It matters to me.'

'Let's just say my boss took care of it.'

Kier glanced over at Ryan, sleeping like a baby on the carpet.

'*Him?*'

Maggot shook his head. 'Oh no. As you can see, Ryan's a bit of an amateur. The man who killed your father is a professional. He doesn't like to miss. And you know what?' He raised the pistol. 'Neither do I.'

Suddenly Kier's mind was filled with images: stars glimpsed through a shattered windscreen, a desperate race through a hospital and a cool ocean in the heat of the day.

Find out what matters and go after it the best way you can.

Kier stared at the circle of the gun barrel and imagined the bullet inside, waiting to be unleashed by a finger's pressure. In a split second everything would be over and his best would never be done.

And because he didn't want that, and because his best was better than Maggot could ever have imagined, Kier reached back and flung the apple from the fruit bowl, diving sideways at the same moment that the gun twitched in Maggot's hand.

As the bullet hit the dressing table, the apple struck Maggot in the centre of his forehead, knocking him backwards and splattering the walls with white pulp. Kier rolled forward, kicked Maggot's legs away and brought him crashing to the floor. As he lay clutching his head, Kier pulled the plastic bag from beneath the bed and removed the washing line. Grabbing the secateurs, he cut a short length of line and pulled Maggot's arms up behind his back. Then he wrapped the line around his wrists and bound them tightly together, securing them with a double knot.

'Hey!' protested Maggot, his voice muffled by the carpet. 'What the hell are you doing?'

'Shut up,' said Kier coldly. 'Just shut up.'

He checked on Ryan to make sure he was still out of it, then picked up the gun, flicked the safety on and pressed the barrel into the back of Maggot's neck.

'Not smiling now, are we?'

Retrieving the brown-paper package from the bed, Kier ripped it open and saw there were several plastic bags filled with white powder. He tore the corner off one of the bags and poured a little pile of powder on to the carpet.

'Doesn't look much, does it?' he said, turning Maggot's face around to look at it. 'But I guess it's enough to keep you in guns and trainers for a while, eh? Am I right?'

Maggot struggled to free his hands from the washing line, but Kier had tied it tightly and Maggot wasn't going anywhere. Realising it was useless, Maggot rested his chin on the carpet and glared at Kier.

'I should have killed you,' he said. 'I should have killed you while I had the chance.'

'Maybe you should,' said Kier, 'but you didn't. So now it's my turn.'

'What do you mean?'

'I mean,' said Kier, lowering the gun barrel and pointing it at Maggot, 'that I'm going to give you a choice.'

'Oh yeah? And what's that?'

'It's very simple. Either you tell me who killed my father or you don't get to tell anyone anything. Ever again.'

'Don't make me laugh,' sneered Maggot. 'You ain't got the bottle for it. You couldn't kill anyone in cold blood, any more than your old man could.'

Kier felt as though someone had twisted a knife in his stomach.

'What?' he whispered. 'What did you say?'

'Your dad had a fight with the guy who killed him a couple of weeks beforehand. When he took the knife off him, he could have finished it right there. But he didn't. And you know why?'

'Because he was a good man, that's why,' said Kier, his voice shaking.

'No,' said Maggot, his eyes focusing on the gun. 'Because he didn't have the backbone. Just like you don't.'

Kier put the gun to Maggot's head and tightened his finger on the trigger.

'Don't make me do it,' he said, his thumb hovering over the safety catch.

Then, because he couldn't trust himself not to flick it off and pull the trigger, he slid the gun under the bed and pulled out the washing line.

'I tell you what,' he said, unwinding the line. 'Let's play a game.'

He sat on the back of Maggot's legs and, ignoring his struggles, wrapped the washing line around them several times before knotting it tightly above his ankles.

'What are you doing?' asked Maggot, suddenly nervous.

He twisted his head around to try and see what Kier was doing.

Ignoring him, Kier tied the other end around the leg of the bed. Then he grabbed Maggot by his jacket and dragged him towards the balcony doors.

'It's a new game,' he said. 'I call it Truth or Dare.'

He pulled Maggot to his feet and pushed him out on to the balcony. Then he tied another length of line to Maggot's belt loop and wrapped the other end around the balcony rail.

'Want to play?'

Maggot struggled, but his hands and legs were tied and Kier held him in a firm grip.

'Get off me,' he said, his eyes flicking nervously

from Kier's face down to the street and back again. 'Let me go.'

'Why would I do that,' asked Kier, 'when we haven't even started?'

He tightened his grip and pushed Maggot closer to the railings.

'OK, here are the rules. I ask you a question and then either you tell me the truth or I dare you to do something. Like, oh, I don't know . . . jump off a balcony, for instance. What do you think? Sounds fun, doesn't it?'

'You're crazy,' said Maggot.

'And the first question is: "Who killed my Dad?"'

'I told you, I ain't telling you nothing.'

'OK, good. Sounds like you're getting the hang of it. So you're going for the dare, am I right?'

Maggot curled his lip.

'Like I said, you ain't got the backbone.'

'OK, ready? I dare you to jump off the balcony. I *double* dare you.'

'I've told you, kid. You don't realise who you're messing with. And if you don't untie me right now, you're—'

'Oh, wait, of course,' said Kier, holding up a finger as if remembering something. 'It's *maggots* that don't have a backbone, isn't it? Well, I guess in that case you're going to need a little help.'

'I don't need your help for nothing,' said Maggot.

'Oh, I think you do,' said Kier.

Then he stuck his foot out, bumped Maggot with his shoulder and flipped his legs up into the air, knocking him over the balcony. As Maggot screamed, Kier grabbed the line that was wrapped around the rail and heard the scrape of the bed as the other line tightened behind him. Just below the balcony, Maggot twisted desperately back and forth, shouting and cursing into the darkness.

'Well done,' called Kier. 'Very good. Now, I'm going to ask you the question once more, and this time I want you to think really, really hard about your answer, OK?'

'OK! OK!' shrieked Maggot. 'It's McIntyre! The guy you want is McIntyre!'

'Who's McIntyre?'

'That's all I know, I swear!'

'Fine,' said Kier, loosening his grip on the line attached to Maggot's belt loop so that he slid further below the balcony. 'Maybe I'll just leave you here while I go look him up in the phone book.'

'Wait!' screamed Maggot. 'He's got a car dealership. Sells top-of-the-range models.'

'Where?'

'Near Morden,' squealed Maggot. 'Just off the Kingston Road!'

'There now,' said Kier. 'That wasn't so hard, was it?'

'Please!' Maggot pleaded. 'Just pull me up!'

But as Kier was about to tie the line securely to the rail, he heard the faintest of clicks and realised three things.

First, that he had forgotten one of the earliest lessons Chiang had ever taught him: *Remain aware of everything.*

Second, that someone was standing behind him.

And third, that the safety catch on the gun had just been flicked off.

TWENTY-TWO

'Move away,' said Ryan. 'Move away from the balcony and put your hands in the air.'

'I can't,' said Kier. 'In case you hadn't noticed, I've got your friend hanging off the end of this line.'

'Move away,' repeated Ryan, 'or I'll blow your head off.'

Kier's mind went into overdrive. He could tell right away that Ryan meant what he said. He just hoped he'd tied the knots on the first line tight enough.

As he let go of the second line there was a piercing scream, the other line hummed like a guitar string and the bed began to slide away from the wall. But although Maggot was heavy, the bed was carved from solid oak. Scraping slowly along the side of the night table, it creaked round a couple more degrees before finally coming to a halt against the dresser. For now at least, the line held.

As Maggot's desperate screams floated into the

night, Kier put his hands up and realised Maggot wasn't the only one running out of options here. Now Ryan knew what Kier was capable of, he wouldn't give him the opportunity to try anything again.

Kier watched him reach for the secateurs, scoop them up and throw them on to the balcony.

'Pick them up.'

'What?'

'You heard me. Pick them up.'

Kier bent down and picked up the secateurs. Then he looked at Ryan, judging the distance.

Ryan saw him.

'Don't even think about it,' he said.

Kier heard the washing line creak and strain under Maggot's weight.

'I think it's going to break,' he said.

'I don't *think* it's going to break,' said Ryan. 'I *know* it's going to break. And the reason I know is because you're going to cut it.'

Kier stared at him in disbelief. He knew that any thoughts of finishing what his father had started, of bringing some justice to the world, would be lost if Maggot fell. He would be responsible for Maggot's death and that would make him a cold-blooded murderer, just like them.

'I thought he was your friend,' he said.

Ryan smiled. 'Friends are overrated. They always want to share your stuff.' He picked up the pile of notes and pushed them into his pocket. 'And I don't like sharing my stuff with no one.'

He took a step closer to Kier and squinted down the gun barrel.

'Turn around.'

Kier turned to face the balcony rail and saw the moon hanging low over the city.

'OK. Cut the line.'

'But I—'

'Just shut up and do it. Cut. Through. The line.'

'But—'

'Argue with me again and I'm pulling this trigger, understand? That's it. Once more and it's over.'

For the first time since arriving back in England, Kier felt utterly powerless: either he cut the line and sent Maggot to his death, or Ryan would shoot him and cut the line anyway. Both ways, Maggot would die. But at least, maybe, if he cut the line, he'd have a chance of saving himself . . .

Kier opened the secateurs and placed the line between the blades.

'Do it!' hissed Ryan. 'Cut the line!'

But at that moment, Kier remembered his father's refusal to kill and something hardened inside him. He might lose his own life, but he wouldn't allow himself to take someone else's.

'No,' he said. 'I won't do it.'

'Fine,' said Ryan. 'Your choice.'

Kier shut his eyes and waited for the world to end. But instead he heard a thud, a groan and then the sound of someone falling heavily to the floor. Slowly, Kier opened his eyes and turned to see Saskia standing next to the now unconscious figure of Ryan. She wore a green, knee-length silk dress with a thick leather belt, suede ankle boots and a simple but very expensive diamond necklace.

'Sorry I'm late,' she said. 'Jackson told me I needed to dress up a bit.' She pinched the hem of her skirt between her fingers, curtsied and smiled. 'What do you think? Do you think I've overdone it?'

Kier looked at her and realised he had never been so glad to see anyone in his life.

'No,' he said. 'I don't think you've overdone it at all.'

Saskia nodded at Ryan, who was still sprawled untidily in the doorway. 'I think you must be losing your touch. That one's softer than a pussycat.' She frowned. 'And what's that washing line doing tied to the bed?'

'Oh *no*,' said Kier, suddenly remembering. 'Maggot!'

He turned to see the washing line slowly stretching like a piece of elastic, pieces of the plastic sleeve pinging off on to the floor.

'Saskia, quick!' he shouted, leaping forward and wrapping the line around his fists. The force of Maggot's weight yanked him off his feet and slammed him into the balcony rail. As the line cut into his hands he cried out in pain, but somehow managed to hold on as Saskia ran across and peered over the edge.

'Who's *that*?'

'Never mind,' gasped Kier, 'just help me pull him up!'

'There's no way we can do that,' said Saskia matter-of-factly. 'He's too heavy.' She leaned further over the rail. 'But he's kind of draped over the balcony down there, so you should be able to hang on while I go and sort him out.'

Kier stared at her.

'While you sort him out?'

'Yeah, shouldn't be a problem. Have you got any more line?'

'Under the bed. But—'

'Just keep hold,' said Saskia. 'I'll be back in a sec.'

Kier gritted his teeth while she knotted one end of the line around the bedpost and tied the other end to her belt.

'See ya,' she said, climbing on to the balcony rail.

Holding the line in both hands, she turned and began abseiling down the wall. After a while Kier felt the weight on the line ease and he was able to stand up and peer over the balcony. Below he could see that Maggot was hanging over the railings like a bag of washing. He watched Saskia swing herself down on to the balcony and then, as she pulled Maggot in after her, the line went slack.

'Throw the line down,' she called.

Kier let go of the line and watched it snake down towards her. She wound it around the rail a few times, tied it off and then sat Maggot with his back against the balcony doors. As she patted his cheek and told him to 'stay there like a good boy', Kier heard him swear and breathed a sigh of relief. He hadn't killed anyone after all.

And now there were two of them to go after the bad guys.

Hearing a groan from the hotel room, he went back inside and saw that Ryan was starting to come round again. He moved quickly, binding his hands with the last of the washing line. Then he tore open the rest of the brown-paper package and shook its contents on to the bed. The top two bags contained a fine white powder, but the others contained a substance that was more granular and slightly creamy in colour. He leaned in for a closer look, then turned to Ryan with his eyebrows raised.

'You wouldn't be trying to rip me off now, would you, Ryan?'

Ryan swore, leaned his head back against the bed and closed his eyes.

'You two really should learn some nicer words,' said Kier.

He took a small foil envelope from his pocket, tore off the corner and removed one of the swabs that Frankie had shown him how to use back in Crete. He rubbed it across the white powder and watched it turn blue, indicating the presence of cocaine.

He winked at Ryan.

'So far so good.'

He took another swab and tested the other powder, but this time, as he had suspected, the swab stayed white. He licked his finger, dipped it in the powder and tasted it with the tip of his tongue. Shaking his head, he tutted disapprovingly.

'You know what I think, Ryan? I think you've been trying to sell me coffee creamer. Which, at thirty pounds a gram, probably makes it the most expensive coffee creamer in the whole world. Wouldn't you agree?'

Ryan shrugged. 'I don't know nothing about that.'

'No, of course you don't. You were just doing your job, weren't you? Just doing an honest day's work, eh, Ryan?'

Kier kept hold of the cocaine and threw the bags of creamer on to the bed. Then he crouched next to Ryan and held up the cocaine.

'You thought you'd sell me a little bit and pocket the thirty grand, didn't ya, big fella? You thought that way your bosses wouldn't know there was a big deal going down. They wouldn't come around demanding their cut of the money. Is that right, Ryan? Is that what happened?'

'Maybe. But now you've got it for free, haven't you? So why don't you just go have your little rich-kid party and get the hell out of my face?'

Kier shook his head. 'You just don't get it, do you, Ryan? I'm not going to any party.'

'But you said—'

'Oh, don't worry. There will *be* a party,' said Kier. 'I'm just not going to be able to make it, that's all.' He waved the packet of cocaine in front of Ryan's face. 'This is pretty good stuff, isn't it? And I know how you love to share your stuff around. So I've decided the party's going to be right here.' He looked at his watch. 'Starts in about ten minutes as a matter of fact. And you and Maggot are going to be the guests of honour.'

'What are you talking about?' asked Ryan. 'There ain't gonna be no party.'

Kier turned to watch Saskia climb over the balcony and untie the line from her belt.

'Ryan doesn't believe there's going to be a party,' he said.

'That's probably my fault,' said Saskia, picking up the gun from the floor. 'I forgot to invite anyone. What kind of hopeless party planner am *I*?'

She picked up the phone and tapped in three numbers.

'Police please. And hurry.'

Kier smiled.

'Yes, hello?' Saskia's voice suddenly became breathy and nervous. 'I'm calling from the Hilton in Park Lane. I'm in room four three six and there are two men here with guns. And I think they're going to, they're going to—'

She aimed the gun at the TV and fired three bullets into it, blowing the screen apart. Then she replaced the phone, winked at Ryan and threw the gun on the bed.

'That ought to do it,' she said.

Kier leaned over and stuffed the cocaine into Ryan's pocket.

'Enjoy your party,' he said.

TWENTY-THREE

McIntyre's Motors (*Cars are our passion*) was a five-minute taxi ride from the station and occupied a large site east of Morden Park. The forecourt was lined with a selection of top-of-the-range cars – Porsches, Ferraris and BMWs – all of them waxed, polished and glinting in the afternoon sunshine.

'Can you wait for us?' asked Kier, handing the taxi driver a twenty-pound note through the hatch.

The driver took the note, held it up to the light and nodded.

'Sure,' he said. 'No problem.'

'Ready?' asked Saskia, slamming the door shut.

'Yeah, let's do it,' said Kier. 'Let's buy a car.'

The salesman was all smiles, smart suit and slicked-back hair.

'Hello, sir, madam,' he said. 'Can I help at all?'

'I think you probably can.'

Kier had detected a slight *touch those cars and*

you're dead kind of tone in the salesman's voice and decided to do something about it.

'My girlfriend's got a birthday coming up in a few weeks and I'm thinking of buying her something a bit special, if you know what I mean.'

'I see, sir.' The salesman looked at Saskia and raised an eyebrow. 'Special birthday, is it?'

Saskia giggled, as if she had temporarily misplaced her brain cells. 'I'll be seventeen!' she said, clinging on to Kier's arm and gazing up at him adoringly. 'Isn't that exciting? I'll be old enough to drive!'

'Yes, you will,' said the salesman. 'Yes, you will.' He smiled thinly, trying to figure out the best way of framing his next question. 'And, um, how exactly were you thinking of funding this purchase, sir?'

Kier beckoned him over, indicating that he had an important secret which he needed to share.

The man leaned in closer.

'My numbers came up,' Kier whispered, 'on the lottery.'

The salesman's eyes widened.

'But don't you have to be eighteen to do the lottery?'

Kier thought quickly. 'Went halves with my brother,' he said. 'Two point five million each.'

The salesman whistled.

'Two point five million, eh? Quite a result.'

'Yes indeedy.' Kier winked at Saskia and flashed her a hundred-kilowatt smile. 'So then, babes. Anything here that catches your eye?'

'Ooh, I don't know,' said Saskia, running her fingers along the bonnet of a Porsche Boxster. 'They're all so shiny and *pretty*.'

'Heh-heh,' said the salesman, pulling out his handkerchief as the strain of smiling brought beads of sweat to his forehead. 'Aren't they though?'

'What's that one over there?' asked Saskia. 'The shiny blue one with the top down.'

'Ah, yes, the BMW convertible,' said the salesman with a knowing smile. 'I see the lady has good taste. Please. Follow me.'

Kier could see that Saskia was enjoying herself. But he could also see her checking out the showroom, looking to see who might be watching.

'Well, here she is,' said the salesman, pointing at the car. 'Do you want to sit in her?'

'Ooh, could I?' squeaked Saskia, all wide-eyed excitement.

'Sure thing, little lady. Just one moment and I'll fetch the keys.'

'I take it he's not our man,' whispered Saskia when the salesman had disappeared off into the showroom.

Kier shook his head. 'No, McIntyre's got to be the

owner. Probably inside counting his money. But don't worry, we'll smoke him out.'

He looked up to see the salesman heading back in their direction.

'Listen, when he gets back, just sit in the car and act dopey while I see what I can find out, OK?'

'OK.' Saskia prepared another simpering smile and aimed it at the salesman. 'This is *so* exciting,' she gasped as he approached. 'I haven't had this much fun in ages.'

Kier smiled at the salesman.

'She doesn't get out much. Too busy counting your diamonds, aren't you, babe?'

'Oh, *you*,' said Saskia. 'He's such a tease, isn't he?'

'Heh-heh,' said the salesman. 'Heh-heh-heh.'

'Could I have a quiet word?' asked Kier, putting his hand on the man's elbow and steering him away from the car.

'Of course,' said the salesman, relieved at not having to laugh any more. 'How can I help?'

'You seem like a man of the world,' said Kier, 'and the thing is, I really want my girlfriend's birthday to be a bit special.'

The salesman nodded enthusiastically. 'A special day for a special lady, eh?'

'Quite,' said Kier. 'The thing is, I'm looking for

something to make her party go with a bit of a swing.'

'A swing?' The salesman frowned. 'I'm afraid I'm not quite with you, sir.'

'I need some of the right stuff,' said Kier, raising his eyebrows, 'or perhaps I should say . . . the *white* stuff.'

Instantly the salesman's face changed. Kier could tell from the glint in his eye that he knew exactly what Kier was talking about. But he wanted to make sure.

'The white stuff?'

'Yeah. You know. Coke. Charlie. Any idea where I could get some?'

The salesman nodded, suddenly serious.

'I might. How much are you looking for?'

Kier decided to go for it. 'It's a pretty big party. How about a kilo?'

'A *kilo*? You're joking, right?'

Kier shook his head and patted his pockets. 'Not with this kind of money. The way I look at it, we're all going to crash and burn some day. Might as well live life in the fast lane while we can.'

The salesman grinned. 'I hear you,' he said, and Kier could practically see the pound signs lighting up in his eyes. 'Just give me a minute, will you? I need to go and have a word with somebody.'

'No problem,' said Kier.

A wave of nausea swept over him as he suddenly realised how close he was to seeing the man who had killed his father. But he reminded himself to stay calm. McIntyre was almost certainly sitting on a big pile of the stuff and finding it would be the perfect way to get back at him. All they had to do was locate the stash, then they could put him away for a very long time.

He walked back to where Saskia was sitting in the BMW, making *Brrm-brrm* noises.

'It's all right,' he said, 'you can knock it off now. He's gone inside to have a word.'

Saskia raised an eyebrow.

'About getting the stuff?'

'Yup.'

'Look. Over there. Do you think that's him?'

Kier turned to see a gold Bentley Continental driving slowly across the car park, its six-litre engine purring like a blender full of cream.

'Damn, it's got to be,' said Kier, angry to have missed it. 'Only the boss would drive a car like that.'

'Don't worry, I'm on to it,' said Saskia jumping out of the car. 'You stay and talk party planning so they don't get suspicious. Soon as I find out where he lives, I'll call you.'

By the time the salesman came scuttling out of

the showroom, Saskia was already climbing into the waiting taxi.

'Is everything all right?' he asked, watching the taxi drive away.

'Everything's fine,' said Kier. 'She just remembered a hair appointment, that's all. Maybe I should buy her a diary too.'

'Is she still interested in the car?' asked the salesman, trying not to sound too desperate.

'Oh yeah, she's made her mind up about that,' said Kier. 'Says it goes with her eyes. Can you believe it?'

The salesman looked relieved. 'So, erm, do you want to put down a deposit?'

'Sure, I'd like to. But to be honest, I didn't think she'd make her mind up that quickly. So I'm going to need to take a trip to the bank. What kind of deposit are you looking for?'

'Say ten per cent?'

'Four grand. OK, that's no problem. And what about, you know . . . our other conversation?'

The salesman glanced around as if he was worried someone might be listening.

'I think we can do you a deal there. Is it still a kilo you're after?'

'Yeah, if the price is right.'

'Tell you what. How about we put the car and

candy together in one package and call it seventy-five?'

'I was thinking more like sixty-five.'

The salesman sucked air through his teeth and shook his head. 'Can't be done, I'm afraid. But maybe we could meet somewhere in the middle.'

'Seventy?'

'Seventy would do it.'

Kier nodded and stuck out his hand.

'You've got yourself a deal.'

As the salesman shook his hand, Kier saw the look in his eyes and realised money was a kind of drug too, pulling you in if you let it.

'I can have it here by tonight,' said the salesman. 'Do you think you'll be in a position to proceed by then?'

Kier nodded. 'You can count on it,' he said.

As Kier walked across the forecourt, the phone buzzed in his pocket. When he took it out he saw that it was Saskia's number and that there was a message.

The message said: *Help*.

TWENTY-FOUR

Kier immediately hit speed-dial but there was no answer. After the third attempt he gave up and called directory enquiries.

'I need the address of M-Taxis,' he told the operator. 'Somewhere in south London, I guess. But can you hurry?'

The cab company turned out to be in a side street close to the station. It was a distance of two miles and Kier ran it in under fifteen minutes.

'Hi,' he said, still out of breath as he entered the office. 'I'm looking for a girl.'

'Aren't we all?' said the stubble-faced man behind the counter.

He looked at his bald, bullet-headed friend and they both laughed unpleasantly.

'You don't understand,' said Kier, leaning on the counter. 'She caught one of your cabs about twenty minutes ago. I need to find out where she was dropped.'

'Maybe you should try saying please,' said Bullet.

Kier wanted to try throwing him through the window, but he held up his hand and said, 'OK, *please*. It's really important.'

'What time did you say she caught the cab?'

'About half an hour ago. It was the same one we caught from the station.'

Stubble Face nodded.

'All right, wait a minute.'

He tapped the computer keyboard and then put his radio headset back on.

'Hi, Andy,' he said. 'Where are you now?'

Kier couldn't hear the response, but something about the way Stubble Face looked at him told him it wasn't the reply he had been expecting.

'OK. And the boy was in the car when you picked them up?'

Kier saw him studying his clothes and his face. He wished he could hear what the other guy was saying.

'Yeah, that's the one. OK, no problem. Leave it to me.'

Stubble Face took off his headset and smiled.

'He says he dropped her off in Richmond. Said she didn't seem to know where she was going.'

Kier began to wonder if perhaps the *Help*

message had been a jokey thing – her way of telling him she'd got herself lost.

'If you come round here I can show you where he dropped her.'

Kier opened the hatch and stood next to Stubble Face, peering over his shoulder at the map.

'See?' said Stubble Face, stabbing an oily finger into the Richmond area. 'Just there.'

But as Kier leaned forward for a better look there was a sudden, vicious pain in the back of his head and then the world went black.

'I think he's coming round,' said a voice. 'Throw some water on him or something.'

Kier saw bright, painful lights and felt as though he was falling. Then someone threw cold water in his face and he opened his eyes to see the blurred features of Stubble Face and Bullet swim into view. He was in some kind of storeroom. Paint was flaking off the walls and a single electric bulb burned above his head.

Kier squeezed his eyes shut and opened them again. He was sitting on a hard wooden chair with his hands tied behind his back.

'Where's Saskia?' he asked.

'Never mind about her,' said Stubble Face. 'It's you we want to hear about.'

'Is this how you treat all your customers?' said Kier, still trying to focus. 'If so, I can't see many of them coming back.'

'That's funny,' said Stubble Face. He looked at Bullet. 'The kid's a comedian.'

'Oh yeah.' Bullet nodded but didn't smile. 'He's a laugh a minute.'

Kier saw he was holding a Micro-Uzi machine pistol, a gun capable of delivering twenty rounds in under a second. Which was definitely not good news.

'What do you want to know about me for? I just came looking for my friend.'

Stubble Face stepped closer.

'Oh, we know what you were looking for. But the question is, who sent you?'

Kier did his best to ignore the pain jumping around in the back of his skull, but it wasn't easy.

'I have no idea what you're talking about.'

'No? Well, maybe I can jog your memory. You see, your little girlfriend made the mistake of asking the driver to follow the car in front.'

'So?'

'So that car was driven by Mr McIntyre, the man who owns this taxi firm and also a local garage. But then I guess you knew that already, didn't you?'

'Why would I?'

'Because, according to the driver, the first place he dropped you was McIntyre's Motors.'

'So I was looking to buy a car. Doesn't make me his best buddy, does it?'

'You ain't old enough to drive a car,' said Bullet.

Kier squinted up at him.

'Who said anything about driving it?'

'Why else would you want one?'

'It was a present for my girlfriend. Listen, when you've got money, you can buy anything you want. But then you probably wouldn't know about that, would you?'

'I'll tell you what I do know, rich boy,' said Stubble Face, leaning in so close that Kier could smell the sweat and cheap aftershave. 'I know you ain't buying your way out of this one. See, when he was driving home, Mr McIntyre got a phone call telling him how two of his guys got turned over at a hotel by a couple of kids.'

Kier was taken aback by this. Who could have told him that?

His surprise must have shown, because Stubble Face grinned.

'Yeah, that's right. And then the weirdest thing happens. He gets another phone call from one of his drivers saying some girl has climbed into his cab and wants to follow his car. Then Mr McIntyre starts getting paranoid. You know what paranoid means?'

'Yeah. It means he thinks people are out to get him.' Kier glanced at Bullet's trigger finger. 'I'm starting to know how that feels.'

'Oh, you ain't felt nothing yet,' said Stubble Face, squeezing his knuckles until they cracked.

Kier didn't much like the sound of that. He also didn't like the fact that he was stuck in here when he should be out trying to help Saskia. This was a mess, no doubt about it.

'Now here's how things are going to work,' said Stubble Face, turning around and locking the door. 'Either you tell us what you and your little friend are up to, or me and *my* little friend are going to break every bone in your body.'

'That's a lot of bones,' said Kier, staring at a spot on Bullet's forehead and trying to remember the finger dislocation thing Chiang had shown him. 'Two hundred and six to be precise.'

He straightened the forefinger on his right hand, slid his thumb underneath and wrapped the other fingers around it. Then he squeezed hard until it clicked.

'In that case,' said Bullet, unfolding the stock of his machine pistol, 'maybe we should get started.'

Kier nodded. 'Maybe we should,' he said.

Then he moved his hands silently through the rope around his wrists, fell forward and brought the chair hard and fast over his head. Although it was an old chair, it had been well put together and didn't actually break until the struts hit the middle of Bullet's forehead. At which point it splintered into several pieces, all of which hit the floor about half a second before Bullet did.

Stubble Face stared at the space where Bullet had been standing, mouth open like a fairground clown waiting for the next ping-pong ball to pop up.

Kier smiled. 'Two hundred and six, remember?' he said. 'Where do you want me to start?'

Stubble Face had been in a lot of fights in his time and knew a lucky strike when he saw one. Now it was time to teach this kid a lesson. Pulling out a telescopic baton, he flicked his wrist and half a metre of hardened steel extended from the palm of his hand. Swiping the air in front of him, he beckoned to Kier and smiled.

'Come on then, rich boy,' he said. *Swish, swish, swish.* 'Let's see what you're made of.'

Kier knew he was made of blood and bones, same as Stubble Face. But while Stubble Face had spent years feeding his body with smoke and junk food, Kier had been learning to make his dance – the kind of dance that Stubble Face could never even begin to imagine. Which was why, when he swung the baton at Kier's head, there was only a *swish* of air, followed by the crack of plaster as the baton struck the wall where Kier had been standing a second before.

When Stubble Face swung the baton again, Kier ducked, thinking of the hours he had spent standing in the centre of the monastery hall, eyes closed, waiting for the air pressure to change around him. He had been knocked over more times than he cared to remember as Chiang swung the ropes with thick wooden logs tied to the end. Sometimes there were five or six of them, all criss-crossing the monastery floor at the same time. But as Chiang was fond of saying, *Pain is the fastest teacher.*

Kier watched Stubble Face swing the baton a third time and then – deciding that enough was enough – he ran up the wall and flipped back on to the man's shoulders with just enough force to unbalance him and send him crashing into the door. As the baton spun away across the floor, Kier picked up the machine pistol and pointed it at the now terrified Stubble Face.

'I need an address,' he said, 'and I need it now.'

'T-twenty-six The Beeches,' stammered Stubble Face. 'Don't shoot! Don't shoot!'

'Postcode?'

'I don't—'

Kier lowered the gun a fraction.

'Postcode?'

'NW3! It's NW3!'

Kier unlocked the door and opened it.

'Sweet dreams,' he said.

Then, as Stubble Face cowered in the corner, he shot out the light, locked the door again and took a set of keys from behind the counter.

'NW3 please,' he said, unlocking the door of the taxi parked in the yard. 'Certainly, sir,' he told himself. 'We'll have you there in no time.'

Then he slotted the key into the ignition, fired up the engine and accelerated away beneath the dark and bloodshot sky.

TWENTY-FIVE

The Beeches was a smart, well-lit cul-de-sac lined, unsurprisingly, with beech trees. Kier could tell by the high walls and the size of the houses that this was an expensive area. Unless garages and taxi firms were suddenly doing incredibly well, McIntyre was obviously making his money from other, more lucrative interests.

Kier parked the car behind some roadworks, stood next to a canvas workmen's shelter and checked his phone for messages. There was only one, a text from Jackson which read: *Update required*.

He deleted it and tried Saskia's number again, but there was still no reply. Slipping the phone back into his pocket, he jogged along the street and checked out the house numbers: 18, 20, 22 . . .

Number 26 stood right at the end of the cul-de-sac and was, by some margin, the grandest house of them all. Spanning the width of the street, it was fronted by a pair of wrought-iron gates and surrounded by three-metre-high walls topped off with razor wire and broken glass. Through the gates, Kier could see a gravel drive bisecting neatly cut lawns and sweeping up to the stone pillars of a mock-Tudor mansion. On either side of the house he could just make out several figures dressed in dark clothing. They stood in the shadows, scanning the grounds and making sure that everything was as it should be.

McIntyre, it seemed, was not a man who liked visitors.

Kier moved away from the gates and looked around. He could see the old stumps of trees that had been deliberately removed from this part of the street and knew he wasn't getting in that way. He stared up at the wire and glass on top of the wall, then ran his fingers over the brickwork searching for some grip. But the surface was too smooth, even for him.

Kier hammered his fist against the wall in frustration. Saskia was here, she had to be. And if McIntyre's employees were anything like the ones at the taxi firm, she was in serious trouble. But there was no way he was getting over that wall any time soon. And he guessed they wouldn't be in a rush to open the gates for him either.

Kier took the phone from his pocket, finger

hovering over the 9. If he called the police now, she might still have a chance. But then he remembered Jackson saying, *Best not to involve them*, and guessed he had his reasons. Besides, a call from some kid on a Pay As You Go would hardly be enough to have them storming the place. Particularly when they found out it was the same kid who'd knocked out one of their officers and stolen one of their police cars.

Kier leaned back against the wall and closed his eyes.

What would Chiang do?

The answer was obvious, of course. Chiang would never have got himself into this mess in the first place.

But as he looked down the street and listened to the breeze rustling the leaves, it reminded him of the sea. He thought of a sun-baked gorge, a silent monastery and the sweetest water he had ever tasted.

We should not let unexpected hardships remove us from the path. If we learn to be patient, to endure, then the things we seek will be sweeter in the end . . .

Kier opened his eyes.

He took a slow, deep breath.

Then he began to run.

Ten metres from the car, Kier pulled the keys from

his pocket and unlocked the doors, still running. When he reached the car, he wrenched the driver's door open, jumped inside and started the engine. Noticing a book of matches stashed in the cup holder, he hurriedly picked them up and put them in his pocket. If the petrol tank burst, he certainly didn't want them flying around.

Revving the engine, he threw his arm over the seat and reversed back up the road, narrowly missing a small dog that came yapping from the shadows.

When he reached the far end of the road, he stopped and tapped the gear lever into neutral. He wiped his forehead and checked that the pavements were empty.

This was it.

It was now or never.

A sudden knock on the side window made his heart skip a beat and he turned to see an old man waving at him.

'What?' mouthed Kier, exasperated.

The man was signalling for him to roll down the window. As the glass slid away he asked, 'Can you take me to Cromwell Street?'

Kier shook his head.

'Not right now, I'm afraid.'

'Why not?'

Kier thought for a second.

'Because this car's going in for repair.'

The old man frowned.

'It looks all right to me.'

'Give it a couple minutes,' said Kier.

Then he wound up the window, slotted the gear lever into place and floored the accelerator.

The car leapt forward in a squeal of burning rubber and Kier let the revs build up just the way Frankie had shown him, allowing them to howl all the way to the limit before changing gear and repeating the process. Halfway down the street, with tyres and motor protesting, he changed up again and watched the speedometer hit fifty. As trees and houses shot past in a blur, he kept his foot planted firmly on the accelerator, gripping the steering wheel tightly in both fists and keeping his eyes fixed on the pair of wrought-iron gates ahead.

'Keep going,' he told himself as the gates rushed towards him. 'You'll be fine.'

Then the front wheels hit the pavement, the tyres burst and sparks flew from the rims before the front bumper smashed into the gates and the bonnet crumpled, the windscreen splintering in a screech of metal and broken glass. For a moment the world seemed shocked into silence, punctuated only by the hiss of steam from the cracked radiator. Then

Kier noticed some white rubber draped across the steering wheel and realised he had just been punched in the face by an airbag.

Staring through the shattered windscreen he saw that he had not, as he had hoped, broken through the gates. Instead they had buckled inwards and the front of the car was now wedged firmly between them. As if that wasn't bad enough, dark figures were running at full pelt towards him and his plan of creating a diversion while he escaped into the shadows of the garden was in definite need of a rethink.

Kier thumped his shoulder against the buckled driver's door and tumbled out on to the pavement. For a moment he looked at the gap between the gates and thought about trying to squeeze through. Then a big-muscled guy with a baseball bat arrived on the other side and Kier decided against it.

'Hey!' shouted the man, pointing the bat at Kier. 'Stay where you are.'

As the man tried to force his way through the gates, Kier struggled to his feet and saw the neighbourhood curtains starting to twitch. He felt bruised and battered, as if he'd been through a tumble-drier full of boulders.

'I said stay where you are!'

'Yeah, I heard you,' said Kier, limping away.

Two more men approached the gates and Kier knew he'd blown it. The crash had hurt a lot more than he'd expected and he knew he didn't have the strength to take all three of them on. As the man with the baseball bat squeezed through the gate, he considered just giving in to it all; just letting the world come and do whatever it was going to do.

'Wait a minute,' said the man. 'You're that kid, aren't you? The one who's been causing all the trouble.'

Kier shrugged.

'Probably,' he said, walking further along the wall.

The man thumped the baseball bat into the palm of his hand.

'Well, how about that? We were just gonna start teaching your little friend a lesson, and then you go and turn up.'

Through his pain, Kier felt a spark of anger crackle in his veins.

'What little friend?'

'Oh, don't tell me you don't *know*. I'm talking about your little girlfriend. She's real pretty, ain't she? But she don't say much.' The man smiled. 'I guess that'll change once me and the boys get started.'

'Don't touch her,' said Kier, imagining the other

men would already be climbing through the twisted gates. 'Don't you *dare* touch her.'

'Oh, I'm sorry,' said the man, 'are you threatening me? Cos if you are, we can start this right now. How would you like that, huh?'

Kier glanced at the wall and took off his jacket.

'I think,' he said, 'I would like that a lot.'

The moment he swung the bat, the man knew something was wrong. The problem was, his mind had become used to the way the world worked. It had become used to the idea of cause and effect, which said that when you swung a baseball bat at a fourteen-year-old kid, the kid went down faster than a henhouse in a hurricane. But in a sudden movement which he couldn't follow or understand, all his ideas got ripped up and blown away; there was a blur, a sharp pain and then he couldn't remember his name or how his legs worked.

As the man fell against the wall, Kier ran up his back and – using his head as a step – threw his jacket over the razor wire and pulled himself up. He watched while the other men squeezed through the gates, then retrieved his jacket and leapt down into the darkness.

TWENTY-SIX

Kier could hear the men on the other side of the wall slapping the guy's face and asking him where in hell the boy had gone.

'I don't know,' the man kept saying. 'I just don't know.'

Pulling on his jacket and keeping to the shadows, Kier crouched low and ran around the side of the house. He reached a courtyard with a large van parked in it. On the side of the van were the words: *Exotic Entrances Ltd – Doors with a Difference*. The back had been left open and, as he peered inside, Kier could see piles of wooden doors stacked across the width of the van. Each door was decorated with brightly coloured paintings of parrots, vines and exotic flowers.

Weird, thought Kier.

McIntyre was obviously a man with his fingers in many pies.

Behind him he could hear movement inside the

house and shouts from the front garden. On the far side of the courtyard there was a long brick building with a flat roof. There were blinds on the windows and the place was in darkness. Kier guessed it was a reasonable place to start. But he didn't have much time.

Running across the courtyard, he tried the door but it was locked. Towards the far end, however, he could see a small window that had been left open for ventilation. It wasn't much, but it was enough.

He took off his shoes and socks and felt the cool stone against his feet.

It was good to be barefoot again.

It reminded him of Chiang.

Pulling out the laces, he tied them together and made a loop with a slipknot at one end. Then he climbed on to the ledge, slid his arm through the open window and let the shoelace drop until it was level with the main window catch.

Behind him the voices were getting closer, but Kier took a deep breath and concentrated on allowing his heart rate to slow, calmly moving his hand until the shoelace hooked over the catch and he was able to pull it sharply upwards.

The main window opened inwards and Kier heard something fall and shatter in the darkness. As he lowered himself into the room he became aware of a sweet, chemical smell which caught the back of his throat, reminding him of the pear drops he used to buy from the corner shop when he was younger.

Reaching into his pocket, Kier pulled out his phone and switched on the torch. The shattered remains of a glass jar glistened in the light and a pool of liquid was spreading out across the floor. Wooden doors lay on top of benches draped in dustsheets, like some kind of ghostly art installation.

As Kier moved closer, he saw that the sheets were covered with tiny curls of wood shavings. A number of aluminium cheese graters were lying around, apparently having been used to scrape the top layers of paint and wood from the doors. Kier stared at the nearest door, which had had most of its top surface removed, leaving only a few painted leaves and a rainbow in the top left-hand corner.

Kier frowned. It didn't make any sense. Why would someone buy a whole load of exotically painted doors only to scrape the surface off again?

He picked up a handful of wood shavings and put them in his pocket. Then he swept the torch around the room and saw that, at the far end, a long bench had been set up with an electric heating plate, on top of which was a large glass flask and a series of tubes leading to a smaller flask in a bath of cold water. It reminded Kier of an experiment they had done at school to separate salt from seawater.

But Kier guessed McIntyre wasn't studying for his GCSEs.

So what kind of experiments was he carrying out here?

A faint noise made Kier spin around and he swept the torch beam across the dustsheets, looking for any sign of movement.

There it was again.

A muffled sound from somewhere in the corner.

Something was moving beneath the sheets.

Kier picked up some wood from the workbench, held the phone between his teeth and crept slowly towards the corner of the room. Raising the piece of wood above his head, he pulled back the dust-sheet, ready to strike. But, to his surprise, he found himself staring at the gagged face of a young girl, bruised and blinking in the glare of torchlight.

'Saskia!' he gasped, ripping off the tape that was plastered across her mouth.

Saskia sat up and coughed into her hand.

'You got my message then.'

'Yeah, I got it,' said Kier, untying the rope around her wrists. 'What happened to you?'

'Taxi driver tasered me,' said Saskia.

'He *tasered* you?'

'Yeah. You know.' She made her fingers into the shape of a gun. 'Zapped me with a stun gun.'

'*Ouch.*'

'Yeah, ouch is right.' Saskia wiped dust from the corner of her eye. 'Took the curls right out of my hair.'

'What happened to your face?'

Saskia rubbed her wrists.

'That was Mr Mac and his mates. They wanted to know where you were and who I was working for.'

'What did you tell him?'

'I told him you were a figment of his overactive imagination. Don't think he believed me though.'

Kier squeezed her hand.

'That was brave of you.'

'Nah, not really. After a few kicks there was a big commotion outside and they all went running off to find out what it was. I don't suppose that had anything to do with you?'

'I owed you one,' said Kier. 'Remember?'

Saskia got to her feet and looked around.

'We should go,' she said. 'They were mad before. But now they're going to be *really* mad.'

'Wait,' said Kier. 'We still need to find out where they're stashing the stuff. If we can do that, we've got him.'

'Kier, it's going to be like a wasps' nest out there,'

said Saskia nervously. 'They'll be buzzing around all over the place. And believe me, that McIntyre is evil. We have to go, Kier. And we have to go *now*.'

'Wait.' Kier picked up the flask from the bench and sniffed it. 'This is really bugging me. It smells like cleaning fluid or something. But why would McIntyre be cleaning doors?'

'I don't know,' said Saskia, 'and right now I don't care. Let's just go, OK? We can't do anything if we're dead.'

But as Kier replaced the flask on the worktop there was a sudden click and the room was flooded with light.

'Stay where you are,' said a voice, and Kier turned to see a middle-aged man standing in the doorway.

The man's thinning blond hair was slicked back with gel and his shirt was unbuttoned beneath a dark suit, revealing a thick, expensive gold chain around his neck. He wore a smaller, matching chain around his wrist which jangled when he moved.

All of these things Kier noticed in the first couple of seconds.

But the thing he noticed most of all was that the man was holding a .357 Magnum revolver loaded with bullets that could punch a hole through toughened glass.

Kier decided he really didn't want to find out what the bullets could do to him.

'Who are you?' Kier asked, still having enough presence of mind to put the phone back in his pocket and press *Record*.

'My name's McIntyre,' said the man, 'and either you take your hand out of your pocket or I'll shoot it off.'

Kier did as he was told and stared in surprise. He had expected McIntyre to be the man from the photograph but – quite obviously – he wasn't.

'I'm guessing you must be Kier West. Am I right?'

'Congratulations,' said Kier. 'You win again.'

The man smiled. 'I always win,' he said. 'Just ask your dad.' His smile grew wider. 'Oh, that's right. You can't, can you?'

A chill ran through Kier's blood.

'So it *was* you,' he whispered. 'You killed my father.'

McIntyre nodded. 'Enjoyed it too. Easy as shooting a rat in a barrel.' He screwed up his face and Kier saw hatred glitter in his eyes. 'But the other rat got away, didn't it? And now it's come sniffing around, ready to go squeaking off and telling the world my business.'

'Your business,' said Saskia, 'is nothing but living off other people's misery.'

'Maybe it is,' said McIntyre, 'but then everyone has a choice in life, don't you think? And if they happen to choose what I offer, then that's up to them.'

'My father didn't choose to die,' said Kier bitterly.

'He chose to get in my way,' replied McIntyre, 'which is the same thing, as you are about to find out.'

'Don't be stupid,' said Saskia nervously. 'The police are going to be here at any minute.'

'I know they are, because I called them.' McIntyre smiled. 'Or rather I called my friend, Chief Superintendent Tyler. Just like I called him about all the other scum on my patch.'

McIntyre saw the surprise on their faces and his smile widened.

'That's right. Chief Superintendent Tyler knows the value of teamwork, you see. I scratch his back, he scratches mine. Perhaps that's why he has the highest crime clear-up rate in England. In fact I hear he's in line for some sort of award. Kind of ironic when you think about it.'

Kier remembered the police's early arrival at the bank robbery, McIntyre getting tipped off about the hotel incident and the fact that the police didn't seem particularly interested in pursuing him. Suddenly everything fell into place.

'You set up the bank robbery?'

'Of course.' McIntyre shrugged. 'Tyler needed something high-profile and some of his men were asking awkward questions. So I gave him what he wanted and he found his men something else to do. Not that they'd have uncovered anything. After all, there's no law against owning a pile of doors.'

McIntyre lifted the gun and pointed it at Kier's head.

'Now remind me, what were we talking about again? Ah yes. Choices.'

Suddenly the smile was gone.

'So go on. Choose.'

Kier swallowed.

'Choose what?'

McIntyre ran his tongue over his lips, like a snake that senses its prey.

'Who shall I shoot first? You or the girl?'

Kier knew McIntyre was a pro. He knew that, however quickly he crossed the room, McIntyre would still have time to squeeze the trigger and blow a hole in him. But then the smell of chemicals caught the back of his throat. He saw the liquid pooling around McIntyre's feet and he came to a decision.

'You look like a gambling man,' said Kier, 'so why don't we flip for it?'

McIntyre shook his head. 'Don't think you're talking your way out of this one.'

'Come on,' said Kier, sliding his hand into his pocket. 'If these are my last few seconds on earth, then let's at least make them interesting.'

McIntyre's eyes narrowed suspiciously.

'Take your hand out of your pocket,' he said. 'Take it out now.'

'Whatever you say,' said Kier. 'You're the boss.'

As he pulled his hand from his pocket, Kier ripped a match from its cardboard book, scraped it along the rough striking panel and threw it to the floor. Before McIntyre had time to understand what was happening, the chemical solvent on the ground ignited, a ribbon of fire shot across the floor and then the pool beneath his feet erupted in a ball of flame.

For a few moments all was heat and chaos: McIntyre screamed as his clothes caught fire, the gun went off and the bullet blew out the light. Suddenly the room was plunged into darkness, lit only by the flames that were engulfing McIntyre.

'Come on!' shouted Saskia. 'Let's go!'

But although part of Kier wanted to see McIntyre burn for what he had done, another part of him knew he couldn't let that happen. His father had chosen not to kill McIntyre for the simple reason that he didn't want to become like him.

Love is stronger than hate, Kier.

He couldn't betray his memory now.

'Kier, leave him!' shouted Saskia.

'No,' said Kier. 'I can't.'

Pushing McIntyre to the ground, he threw himself on top of him and spread himself wide, desperately trying to smother the flames. The heat burned his skin as they rolled and struggled, the smell of smoke and scorched clothing filling the room. Then McIntyre twisted, rolled on top of Kier and pulled out a knife. And at that moment, Kier was afraid because he knew it was over and there was nothing he could do. But as McIntyre raised the blade above his head, Saskia's foot flashed through the air and the knife clattered off into the corner of the room. Still spinning, she kicked McIntyre hard in the chest, slamming him against the wall. As he slumped forward, Kier saw flames flicker across the floor and begin to lick at the legs of the benches.

'*Now* will you come?'

As Saskia pulled him to his feet and kicked open the door, Kier ran back, grabbed the semi-conscious McIntyre and dragged him out into the courtyard.

'Leave him!' shouted Saskia. 'Just leave him!'

They were halfway across the lawn when they saw blue lights flashing outside the gates.

'We've got visitors,' said Saskia.

Kier noticed that the van full of doors had been hurriedly driven into the shadows and was now half-hidden behind a tree next to the wall.

'Damn it,' he said as he heard the sound of barking. 'They've brought dogs.'

Two police officers were walking across the grass towards them, their torch beams criss-crossing in the warm night air. In front of them, two large Alsatians growled and strained at the leash.

'Hey!' shouted one of the officers. 'Stay there!'

Saskia looked at Kier.

'What do you think? Should we run?'

Kier shook his head.

'We'll never beat the dogs. But maybe McIntyre was bluffing – maybe the neighbours called them. Maybe we should tell them what we know.'

'We can't, Kier, not without admitting who we are.' Saskia sounded desperate. 'And we can't prove a thing.'

'In that case,' whispered Kier, 'you'd better think of something quick.'

The police officers stopped in front of them, holding the growling dogs by their collars.

'Don't mind us,' said Kier. 'We were just leaving.'

'I don't think so.' The larger policeman studied Kier suspiciously. 'I don't suppose you'd happen to know anything about the car out front?'

'Nope,' said Saskia. 'Absolutely not.'

The policeman kept his eyes on Kier.

'Well, that's funny,' he said, 'because we've been speaking to an old man who said he saw a boy of about your age driving down the street at around seventy miles an hour.'

'Seventy miles an hour?' said Kier. 'No *way*. It was sixty-five, tops.'

'Right,' said the policeman. 'So it *was* you.'

'My friend's life was in danger,' Kier replied. 'What would you have done?'

'Take no notice of him, Officer,' said Saskia, glancing sharply at Kier. 'He's still in shock. He doesn't know what he's saying.'

'Yes, I do,' said Kier. 'The man who lives here is—'

'A respectable businessman,' interrupted a voice, and Kier turned to see a dishevelled McIntyre standing behind him. 'Good evening, Officers.'

The policeman looked him up and down.

'And who might you be?'

McIntyre pushed past Kier and brushed dirt from his jacket.

'I am the owner of this house and I found these two hooligans setting fire to my property. And you say they crashed a car into my gate as well?' He sighed and shook his head. 'I don't know what the world is coming to, Officer, I really don't. Ah,' he added, turning and raising his hand. 'Here's someone who can help us clear this up.'

Kier turned to see a tall, wiry police officer walking towards them. He had silver crowns on the shoulders of his uniform. He also had a moustache. For a moment, Kier wondered why he looked so familiar.

Then it dawned on him.

He was looking at the man from the photograph.

'Chief Superintendent Tyler,' said McIntyre, holding out his hand. 'So good of you to come.'

Kier watched Tyler nod and shake McIntyre's hand, saw how he was ready to back up all his lies and knew there was no point in trying to explain anything.

'All right, you two,' said one of the other officers, reaching for his handcuffs. 'I think you'd better come with me.'

Saskia looked at Kier and then at the police officer.

'That's not going to happen,' she said.

At the same moment there was a loud explosion, the sound of breaking glass and an orange fireball rolled out of the windows into the courtyard behind them.

McIntyre, Tyler and the police officers ducked and covered their heads.

Kier and Saskia turned and ran.

'Not that way!' shouted Kier as another police car screeched to a halt outside the gates.

Saskia immediately changed direction and began running towards the trees. As Kier followed, he saw she was heading straight for the van parked next to the wall. Behind him he could hear the spit and crackle of flames, their long shadows flickering eerily across the grass.

'Over there!' shouted McIntyre, as the dogs barked and pawed at the ground.

Saskia wrenched the van door open, stood on the passenger seat and clambered on to the roof. Kier turned to see a police dog running towards him, ears flat against its head as it sped across the lawn.

Throwing himself into the van, he waited until the dog leapt before kicking the door open again. He was rewarded with a loud metallic clang, followed by a strangled yelp as the dog bounced back on to the grass. Kier grabbed the door frame, swung himself up and somersaulted on to the roof.

'Wait,' he said as Saskia began climbing towards the broken glass and razor wire. He took off his jacket and threw it on top of the wall.

'*Now* go,' he told her.

Glancing down, he saw the four men standing on the grass looking up at him.

'All right, son,' said one of the officers. 'Don't do anything stupid.'

'I wasn't planning to,' replied Kier. He stared at Tyler and McIntyre. 'This isn't over,' he said, 'not by a long shot.'

Then he turned and scrambled up on to the wall next to Saskia.

'OK?' she asked.

Kier nodded.

'Go,' he said.

Saskia took his hand and lowered herself towards the pavement, walking down the wall on the balls of her feet. When Kier's arm was at full stretch, she let go and dropped with a thump. Seeing the police officers turn and run towards the gate, Kier hooked his blazer over the broken glass and jumped after her. There was a tearing sound as the material ripped, but it slowed him enough to ensure he landed in one piece.

'Keep going!' he shouted, chasing after Saskia as she raced past the gate where the police car was parked.

He heard angry shouts and then the squeal of tyres as the car reversed away from the kerb before accelerating down the street towards them. Another police car appeared at the far end of the road, siren wailing and blue lights flashing. It screeched to a halt and two more officers jumped out, cutting off their exit.

'I think we've had it, Kier,' said Saskia, looking around breathlessly. 'They've got us trapped.'

'No, they haven't,' said Kier. He turned to see that the dog handlers had slowed right down, believing there was nowhere else for them to run. 'Quick. In here.'

Grabbing Saskia's hand, he dragged her past the roadworks and into the workmen's shelter. Dropping to his knees, he pulled up a heavy manhole cover and pointed into the darkness.

'Go,' he whispered. 'Go, go, go!'

For a moment, Saskia stared at him as though he was crazy. Then, without a word, she stepped on to the top rung of the ladder and disappeared down into the sewer.

The dogs were close now. Kier could hear their low growls and the scratching of their claws across the pavement.

'Where did they go?' someone shouted.

Dropping down into the hole, Kier slid the cover over his head and the sounds from the street instantly disappeared, as if someone had pulled the plug on a radio. They were replaced by the faint shuffle of Saskia's footsteps in the darkness below.

'It *stinks* down here,' she called, her voice

echoing around the cavernous space. 'Where are we anyway?'

Kier screwed up his nose and smiled.

'Right where we always are,' he said. 'But try not to step in too much of it.'

By the time they found an exit hole several hours later, Kier was down to his last few matches. As he cautiously stuck his head out into the road, he saw that the sky was starting to lighten in the east.

'Look,' he said, taking hold of Saskia's hand and pulling her out. 'I think it's going to be a beautiful day.'

Later, as they sat in a coffee bar and watched the city coming alive, Saskia said, 'I'm sorry we didn't get to put McIntyre away, Kier. I know how much you wanted it. But that's just life, isn't it? I guess you can't win them all.'

'I guess not,' said Kier.

He took a sip of espresso and smiled.

'What?' said Saskia.

'Nothing,' he said. 'Nothing at all.'

Then he dialled the number he'd got from directory enquiries and his smile widened.

'Who are you ringing?' Saskia asked.

'Just an old friend,' he said.

The sergeant on reception wasn't too helpful at first, but when Kier filled him in on the details of when they'd last met, he went and fetched Constable Doyle pretty quickly.

'I'm phoning to apologise,' Kier explained, winking at Saskia, 'for knocking you out and stealing your police car.'

There was a long silence on the other end of the phone, then Doyle asked, 'So what's your plan? Are you going to turn yourself in?'

'Not exactly, no.'

'Then why are you ringing?'

'Like I said, I wanted to apologise. But I've also got some information which you might find useful.'

'I see.' The tone of Doyle's voice suggested that he thought this highly doubtful. 'And what kind of information might that be?'

'Last night there was an incident over at The Beeches. A car crash, explosion, that kind of thing. Couple of kids causing problems for a local businessman apparently.'

'Is that so?'

'That's what I heard. Poor guy was just minding his own business. Running his little car empire and importing a few doors.'

'Listen, son, I'm a busy man.' Kier heard the

exasperation creeping into the officer's voice. 'What's your point exactly?'

'My point,' said Kier, 'is that he's got a van full of doors you might want to take a closer look at.'

'And why would I want to do that?'

'Because it's my belief that they're all soaked in cocaine.'

'Your *belief*? Oh yeah, OK. And you expect me to take your word for that, do you?'

'Not really, no. That's why I'm going to send you a package with some wood shavings in it, so you can take a look for yourself. All you need to do is get them analysed. And if you find out I'm telling the truth, then you might want to give this McIntyre guy a hand to strip a few of his doors down.'

'Why are you telling me this?' asked Doyle.

'Because you tried to help me, remember?' said Kier. 'And now I'm trying to help you. But I'd keep it between you and the anti-corruption unit until you've got some evidence in the bag.'

'What do you mean?'

'I mean you were right when you said Chief Superintendent Tyler is only interested in fixing his crime figures. And believe me, he doesn't care how he does it.'

'Wait. Are you suggesting he's involved in this?'

'I'm doing more than suggesting it. I've got a

recording to prove it. Your Chief Superintendent is in this up to his neck.'

'That's a very serious allegation,' said Doyle, lowering his voice. 'Why should I trust you?'

'Because, believe it or not,' said Kier, 'we're both on the same side.'

He closed the phone and smiled.

'You know what?' he said. 'I think we've got him. I think our friend McIntyre is finally going down.'

'I don't get it,' said Saskia, shaking her head. 'How do you know about the doors?'

Kier poured a tube of sugar into his espresso and took a sip.

'I thought to myself, "Why does a guy like McIntyre go to all the trouble of importing exotic doors only to grind them up into sawdust?" Then, when I smelt those chemicals, it got me thinking.'

'About what?'

'About solvents. Highly flammable ones. Probably not a good idea to chuck a match on them, come to think of it.'

Saskia frowned. 'What are you talking about, Kier?'

'All right, listen. McIntyre knows he can get cheap cocaine in Colombia and sell it for a fat profit in the UK, right?'

'Right.'

'But he also knows that customs officers are going to be paying special attention to anything that arrives from that part of the world. So he arranges to have some doors delivered. When they arrive at customs, the officers X-ray them for hidden drugs but can't find any. Although they're suspicious, there's nothing they can do. So they let them through and McIntyre gets clean away with it.'

'Away with *what?*'

'With a whole shipment of cocaine. Don't you see? The cocaine is dissolved in liquid, which is then soaked into the doors, so that when they go through customs there's no sign of it. But when McIntyre's gang get hold of it, they shave the wood off and drop it in a solvent, which dissolves the cocaine again. Then all they need to do is evaporate the liquid and they're left with one hundred per cent pure cocaine. It's just simple science – separating liquids and solids, same as we do at school.'

Saskia shook her head in amazement.

'That's incredible.' She smiled. 'Bit of a science swot at school, were we?'

'Yeah.' Kier paused. 'You know, I've been thinking a lot about that lately.'

'About school?'

'About that, and about something my dad said to me . . . you know, before all this happened. He told me to find out what matters and go after it the best way I can.'

'Well, you did, didn't you? That's exactly what you did do.'

'Yeah, I know, but . . .'

'But what?'

'But that was just something I had to do, Saskia. And now it's done, I don't want to live in a world where people are trying to kill each other all the time. I want to go back.'

'Back where?'

'To my old life. I want to go back to school. Maybe then I'll find out what really matters.'

'But you can't, can you? Not after this.'

'Why not?'

Saskia put her arms on the table and leaned forward, lowering her voice.

'Because you're too good at it, Kier. Jackson won't want to lose you.'

'Well, he's going to have to. I can't do it any more, Saskia. I just want to be ordinary again.'

Saskia squeezed his hand.

'Trust me,' she said, 'ordinary is one thing you'll never be.'

Then she got up and walked into the cafe.

It was twenty minutes before Kier realised that she

wasn't coming back. As he went to pay the bill, the waitress handed him a folded napkin with his name written on it in blue ink.

'That girl you were with,' she said. 'She left it for you.'

Kier opened it and smiled.

Inside Saskia had written:

In case you can't find what you're looking for.

x

Sellotaped beneath it was a gift card from Harrods.

TWENTY-SEVEN

There were still a few days before the start of term and Kier spent them quietly walking in the park, giving his smart clothes to a charity shop ('Are you sure about this, dear?') and buying some new school uniform.

Before catching the train back to school, he made a quick stop at Pizza Hut.

'Do you deliver?' he asked.

'Sure,' said the man. 'Where did you have in mind?'

It cost him the best part of fifty quid but it was worth it.

Kier imagined the delivery van pulling up by the bridge and the guy getting out with a big stack of pizza boxes. He imagined him walking past the river towards the soup kitchen, peering into the shadows and calling, 'Nuggy? Nuggy? Did anyone here order pizzas with extra anchovies?'

He guessed Nuggy would appreciate that.

On his way to the station, he came across a news-agent's beneath the stone arch of a railway bridge. There were papers on display outside and he picked up one with the headline:

LOCAL BUSINESSMAN ARRESTED IN MAJOR DRUGS BUST: POLICE CHIEF UNDER INVESTIGATION

He was about to walk in and pay for it when he glanced through the window and saw two men standing at the counter. They were wearing thick coats and Kier noticed they had their hoods up, even though it was a hot day. The shopkeeper was shaking his head and waving his hands around, and as Kier looked at the men again he saw that one of them was holding a knife.

'Oh no,' he said, returning the paper to the display stand. 'No way.'

He took a step back and began walking towards the station.

It was nothing to do with him any more.

He was going back to school and that was an end to it.

No more nonsense.

He made it as far as the corner of the street before turning round again.

When he reached the shop, he peered through the glass and saw that one of the men had the shop-keeper by the throat, while the other one emptied the till.

Kier hesitated for a moment and looked at his watch.

Then he took a deep breath, sighed and pushed the door open.

'Hello,' he said. 'Is there a problem?'

READ MORE THRILLING BOOKS BY STEVE VOAKE

OUT NOW . . .

STEVE VOAKE

BLOOD
HUNTERS

THEY KNOW WHERE YOU ARE

Don't turn around . . .

The Mexican jungle: a team of British scientists explore the world's deepest lake. What they discover could wipe out mankind.

England: Joe McDonald's father is arrested for the murder of a fellow scientist and Joe is determined to prove his innocence.

But across town more people are being attacked – in their homes, in the woods, by the canal.

Was something smuggled back from Mexico? One thing is certain: there are predators out there.

Hungry. Intelligent. Unstoppable.

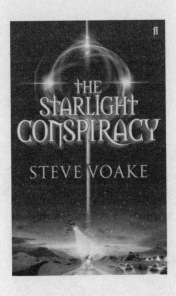

Alone and on the run from Social Services, fourteen-year-old Berry has nowhere to go. Until she meets an old man who entrusts her with a mysterious item that he claims has unbelievable powers. Her life is about to change forever.

A terrorist group and the FBI want the item and will stop at nothing to get it. And soon, Berry and fellow outcast, Elliot, find themselves in a desperate race across the Atlantic to America. From dodging bullets and escaping capture to being hunted through cities and over deserts, Berry must stay alive long enough to find the item's rightful owner – whoever, or whatever, they may be.

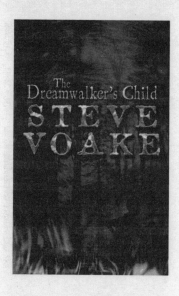

Sam Palmer hates living in the country – he doesn't have any friends and life is dull. Until a bizarre bicycle crash leaves his body in a coma. Now he has far bigger problems.

Sam wakes in Aurobon, a world similar to his own, and discovers that his accident was part of an elaborate abduction. Dark forces led by the brutal Odoursin need him for a deadly agenda, one that threatens to reach beyond Aurobon and into his own world. Aided by the fearless Skipper – an adrenalin-loving girl pilot – and on the run from insects the size of fighter jets, Sam must join the fight against Odoursin and find a way to return home. That's if the terrifying marsh dogs don't kill him first.

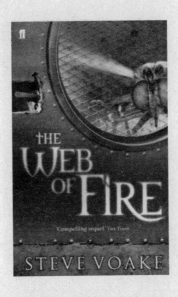

Sam and Skipper are back. But the Aurobon they return to is vastly different from the one they left. Odoursin now rules Auboron, Vahlzi is in ruins, and all that remains of Firebrand's forces are a few resistance fighters.

Sam and Skipper's only hope of fighting Odoursin lies in tracking down a powerful weapon – a search that will take them beyond Aurobon and into a living nightmare. But their mission becomes urgent when they discover that Odoursin is again plotting to destroy humankind – this time by using the President of the United States.